NIGHT AIR

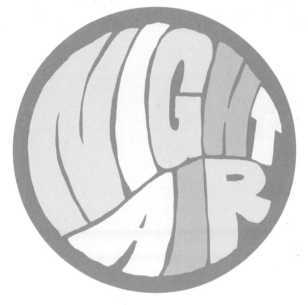

A DOUBLE+ ADVENTURE

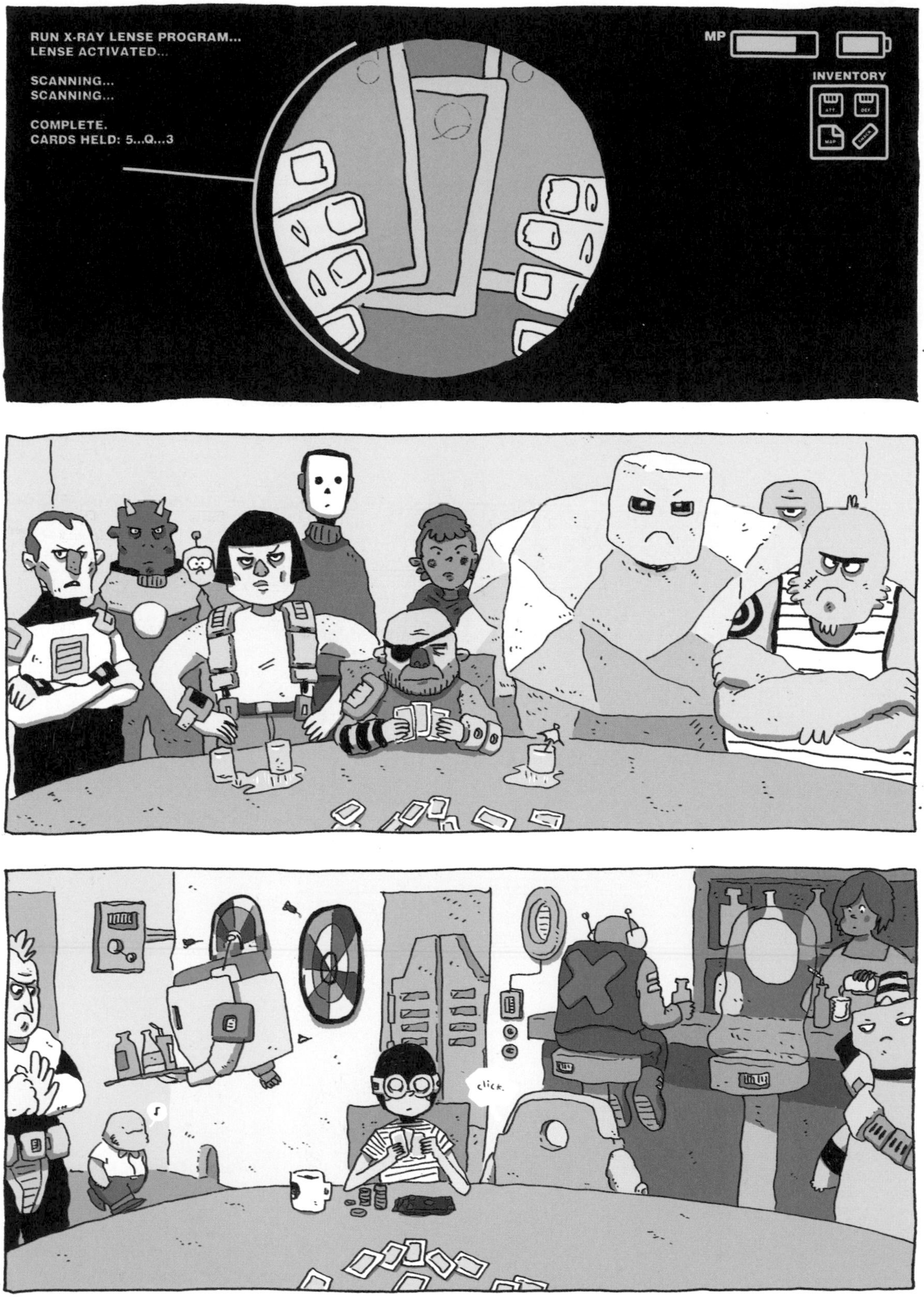
RUN X-RAY LENSE PROGRAM...
LENSE ACTIVATED...
SCANNING...
SCANNING...
COMPLETE.
CARDS HELD: 5...Q...3
MP
INVENTORY
ATT.
DEF.
MAP
SNACK
click.

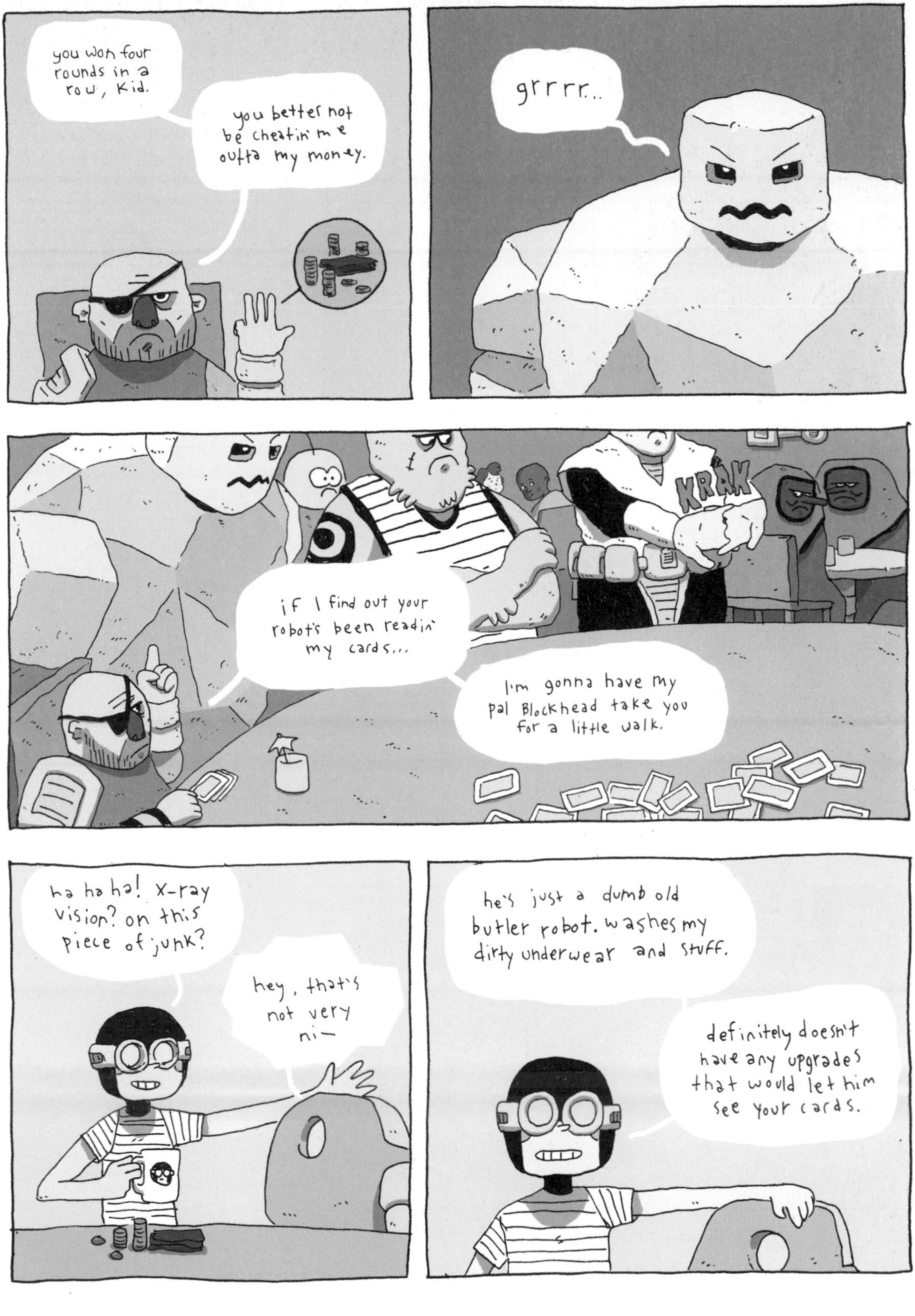
you won four rounds in a row, kid.
you better not be cheatin' me outta my money.
grrrr..
KRAK
if I find out your robot's been readin' my cards...
I'm gonna have my pal Blockhead take you for a little walk.
ha ha ha! x-ray vision? on this piece of junk?
hey, that's not very ni—
he's just a dumb old butler robot. washes my dirty underwear and stuff.
definitely doesn't have any upgrades that would let him see your cards.

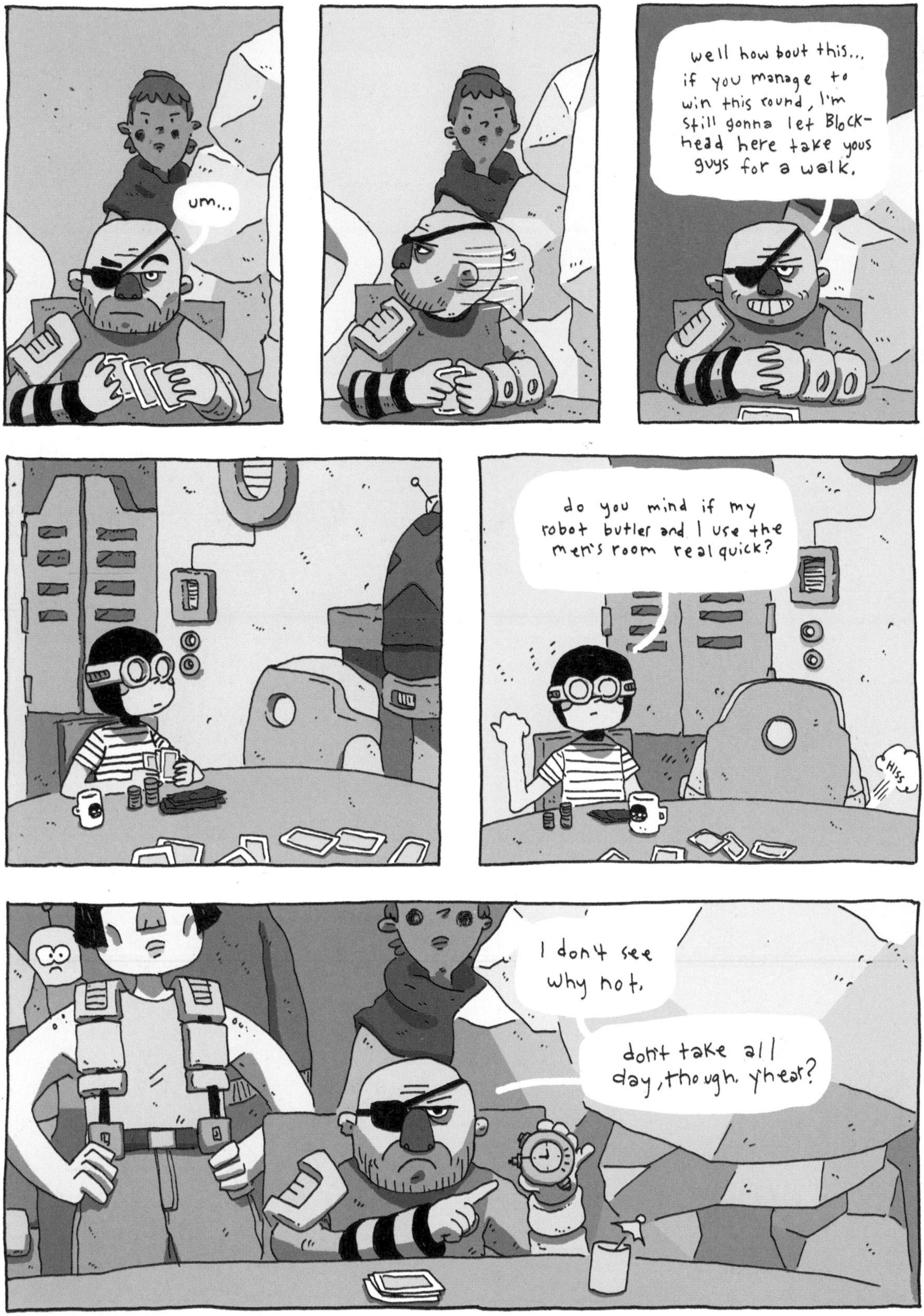
um...
well how bout this... if you manage to win this round, I'm still gonna let Block-head here take yous guys for a walk.
do you mind if my robot butler and I use the men's room real quick?
HISS
I don't see why not.
don't take all day, though. y'hear?

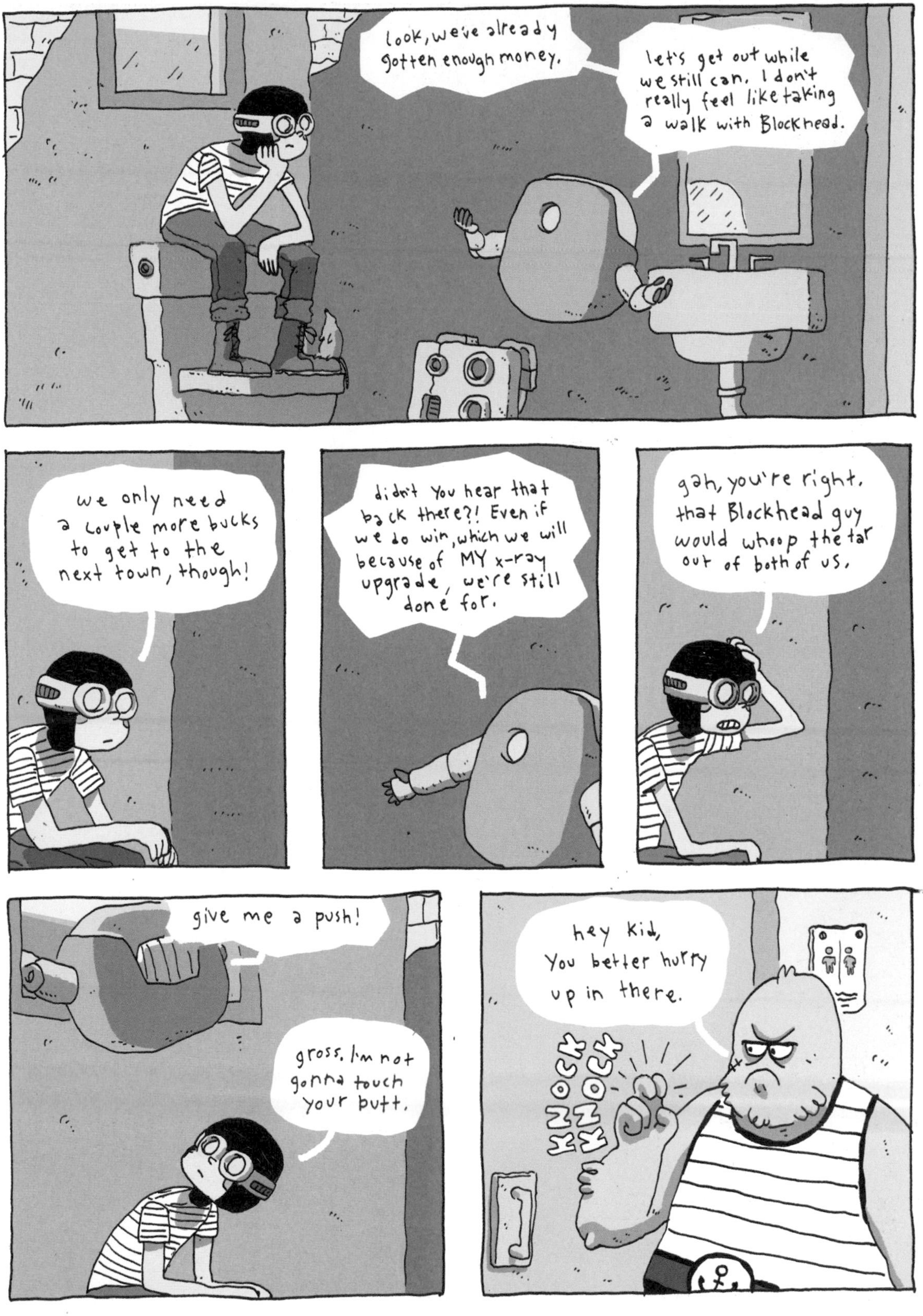
look, we've already gotten enough money.
let's get out while we still can. I don't really feel like taking a walk with Blockhead.
we only need a couple more bucks to get to the next town, though!
didn't you hear that back there?! Even if we do win, which we will because of MY x-ray upgrade, we're still done for.
gah, you're right. that Blockhead guy would whoop the tar out of both of us.
give me a push!
gross. I'm not gonna touch your butt.
hey kid, You better hurry up in there.
KNOCK KNOCK

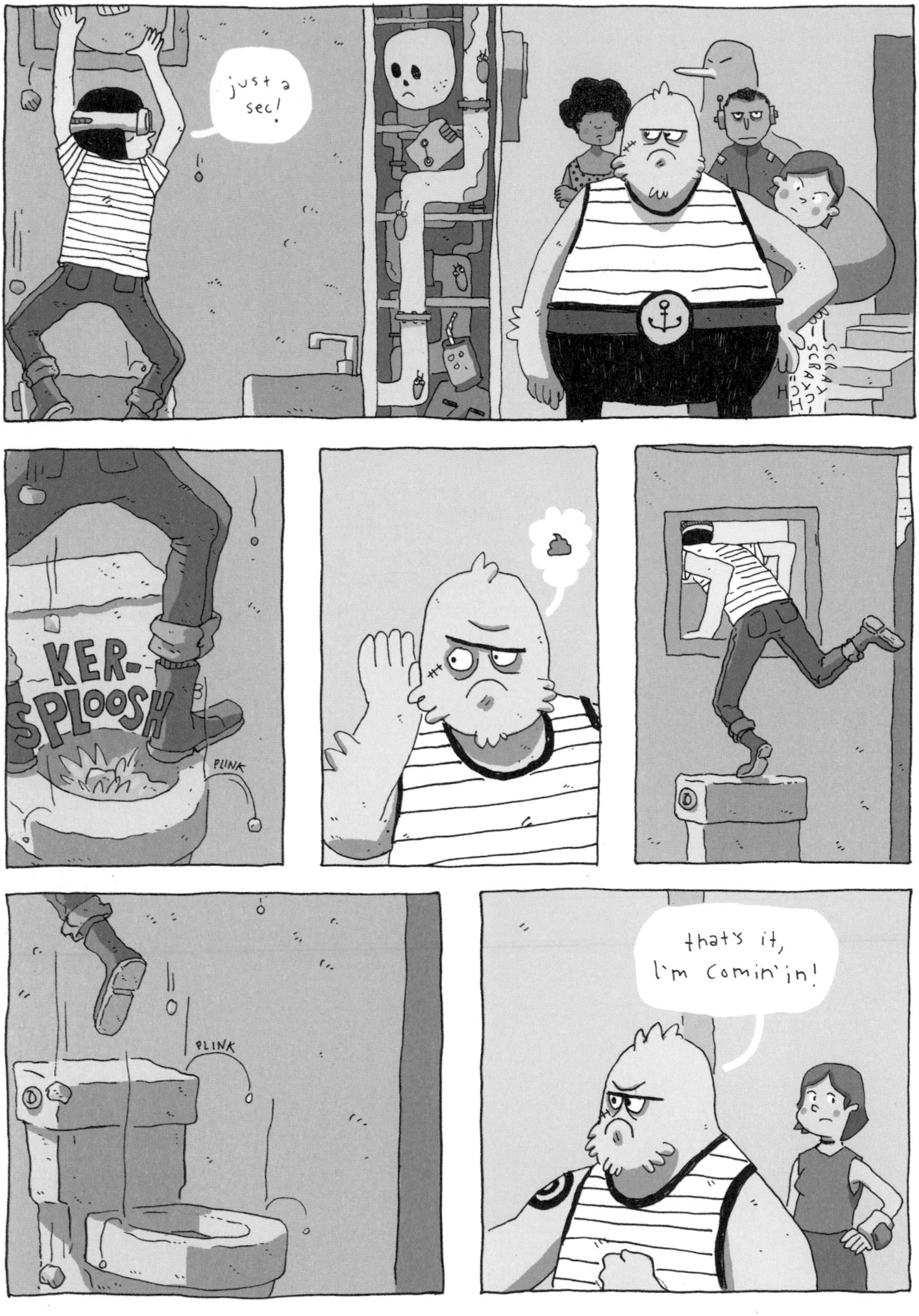
just a sec!
SCRATCH—SCRATCH—SCRATCH—
KER-SPLOOSH
PLINK
PLINK
that's it, I'm comin' in!

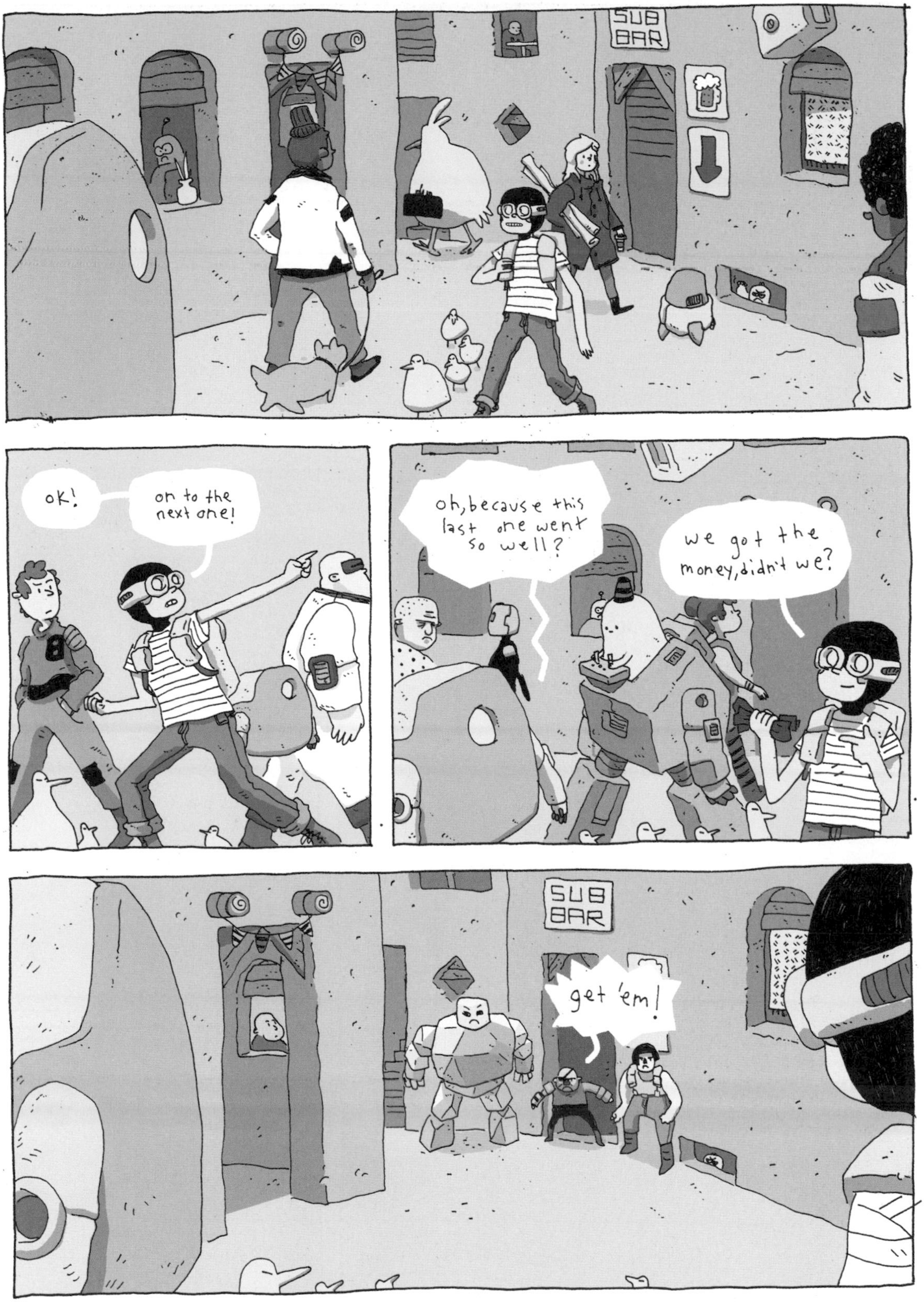
SUB BAR
ok!
on to the next one!
oh, because this last one went so well?
we got the money, didn't we?
SUB BAR
get 'em!

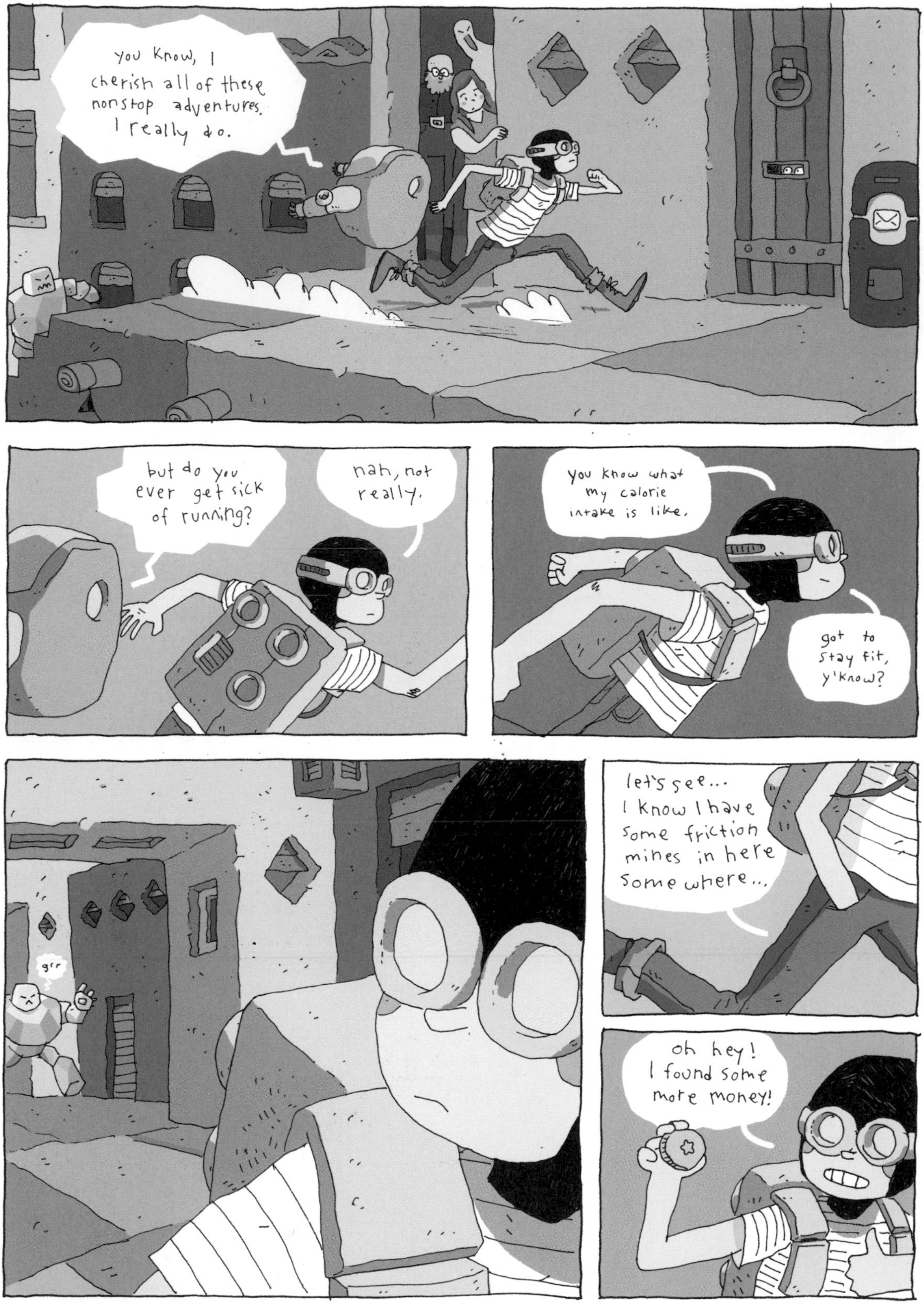
you know, I cherish all of these nonstop adventures. I really do.
but do you ever get sick of running?
nah, not really.
you know what my calorie intake is like.
got to stay fit, y'know?
grr
let's see... I know I have some friction mines in here some where...
oh hey! I found some more money!

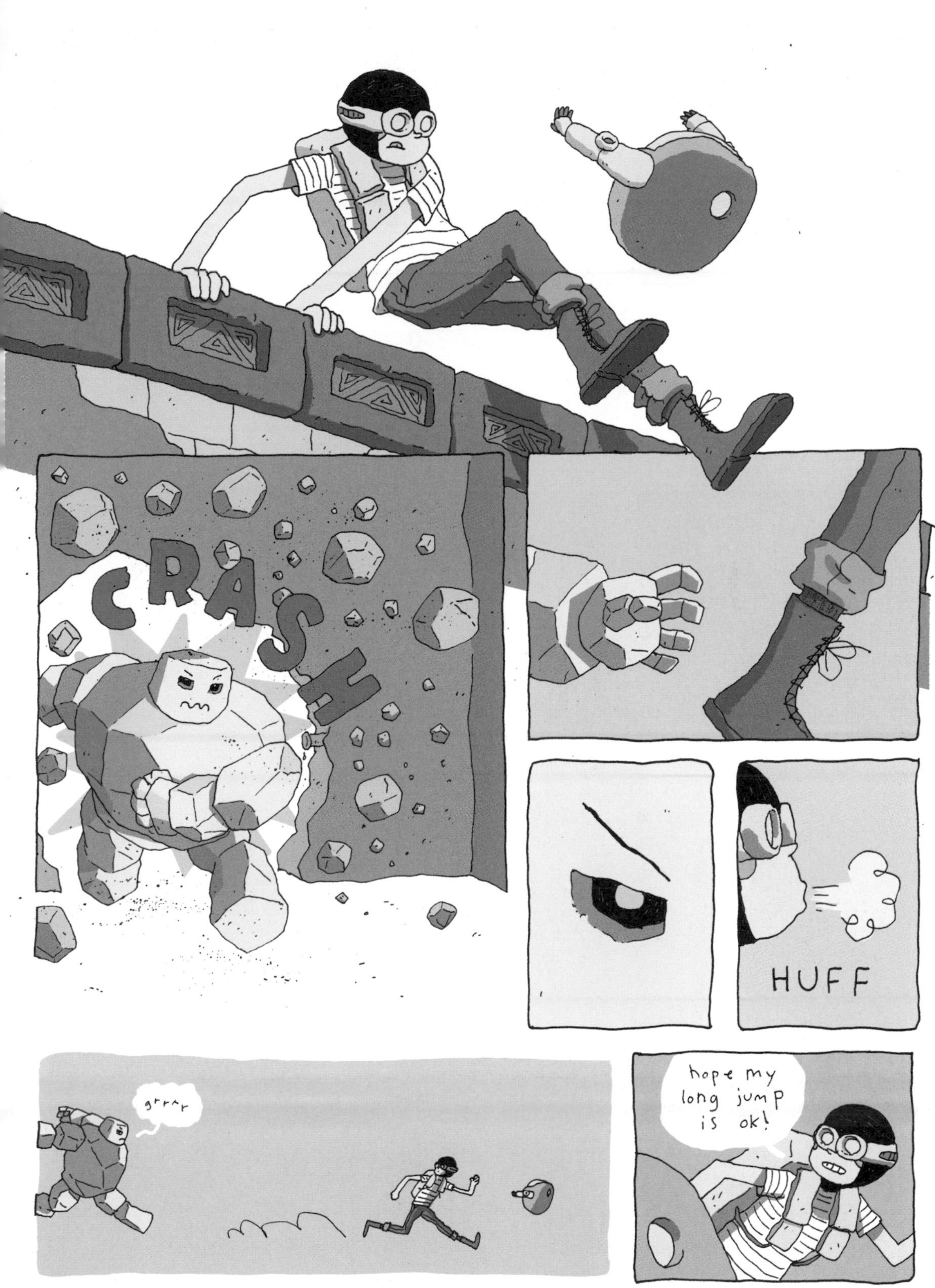
CRASH
HUFF
grrrr
hope my long jump is ok!

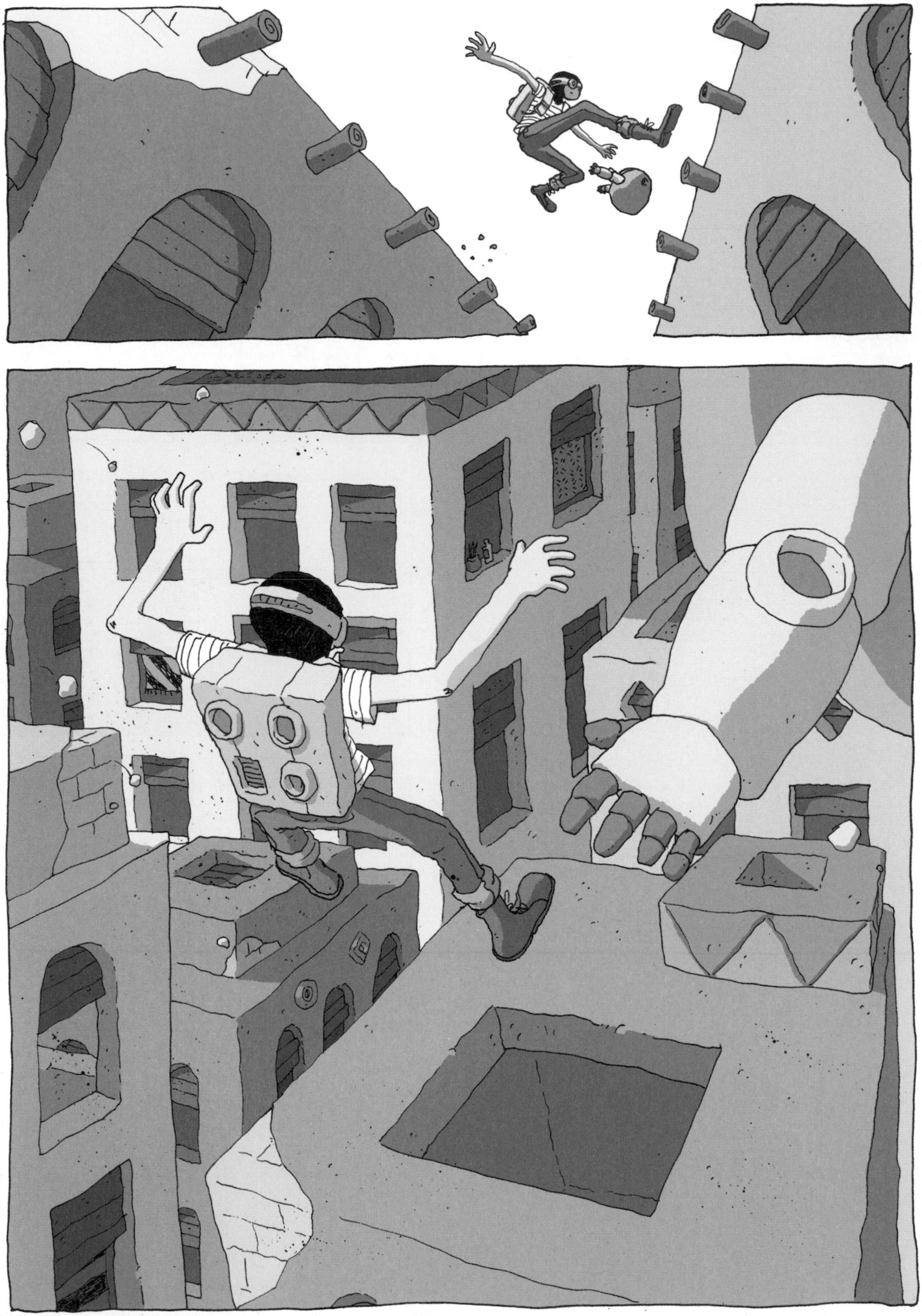

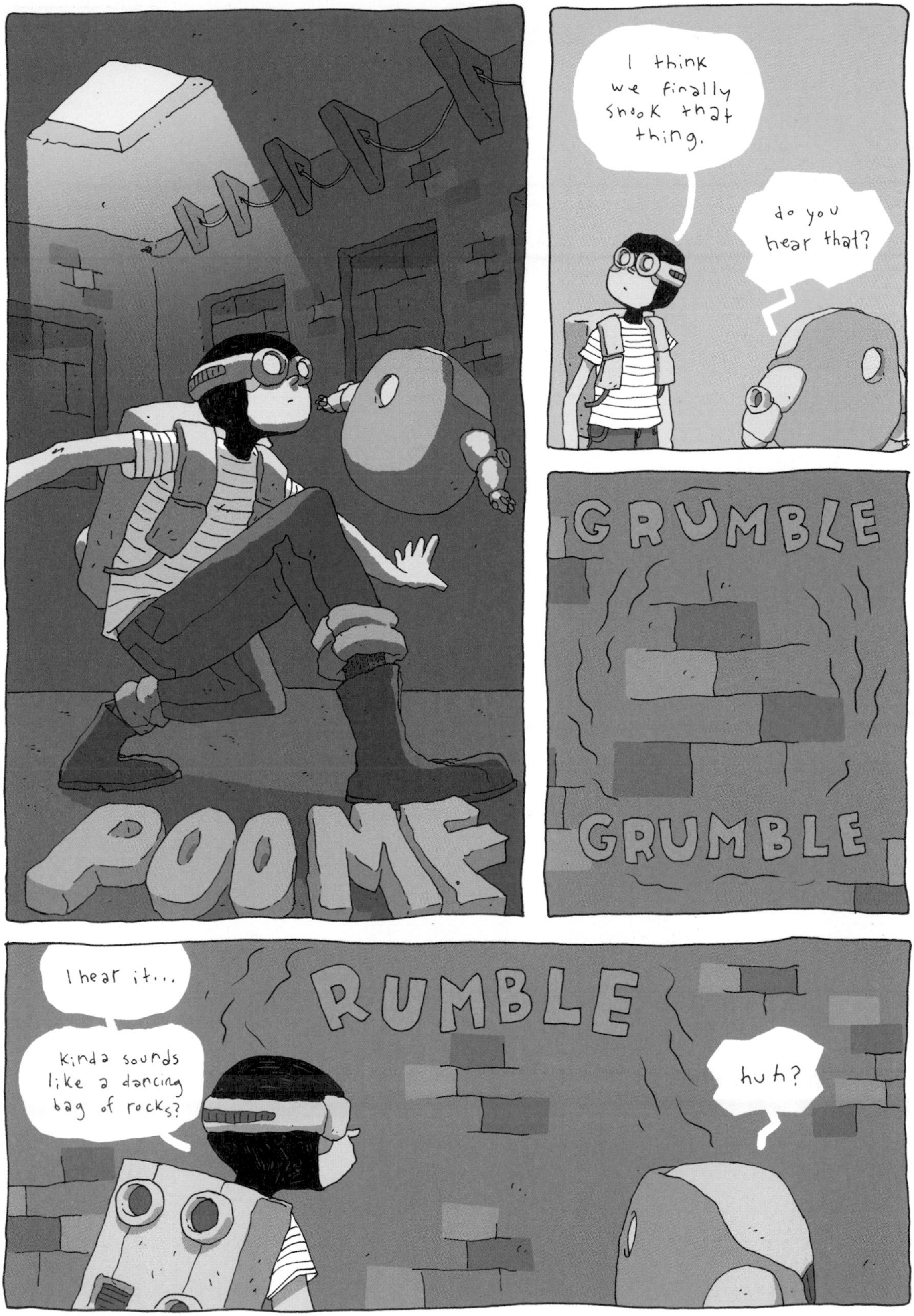
POOMF
I think we finally shook that thing.
do you hear that?
GRUMBLE
GRUMBLE
I hear it...
kinda sounds like a dancing bag of rocks?
RUMBLE
huh?

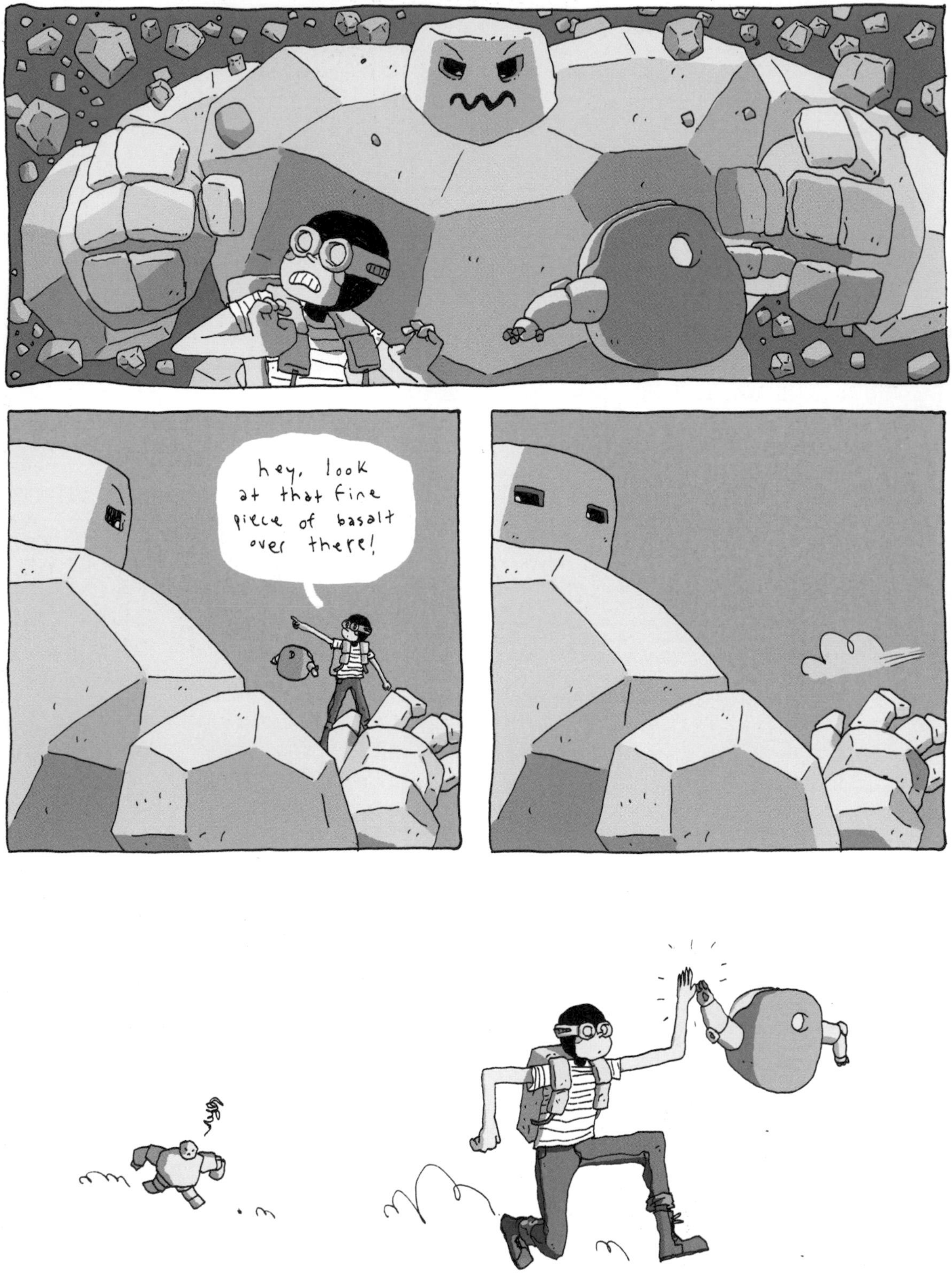
hey, look at that fine piece of basalt over there!

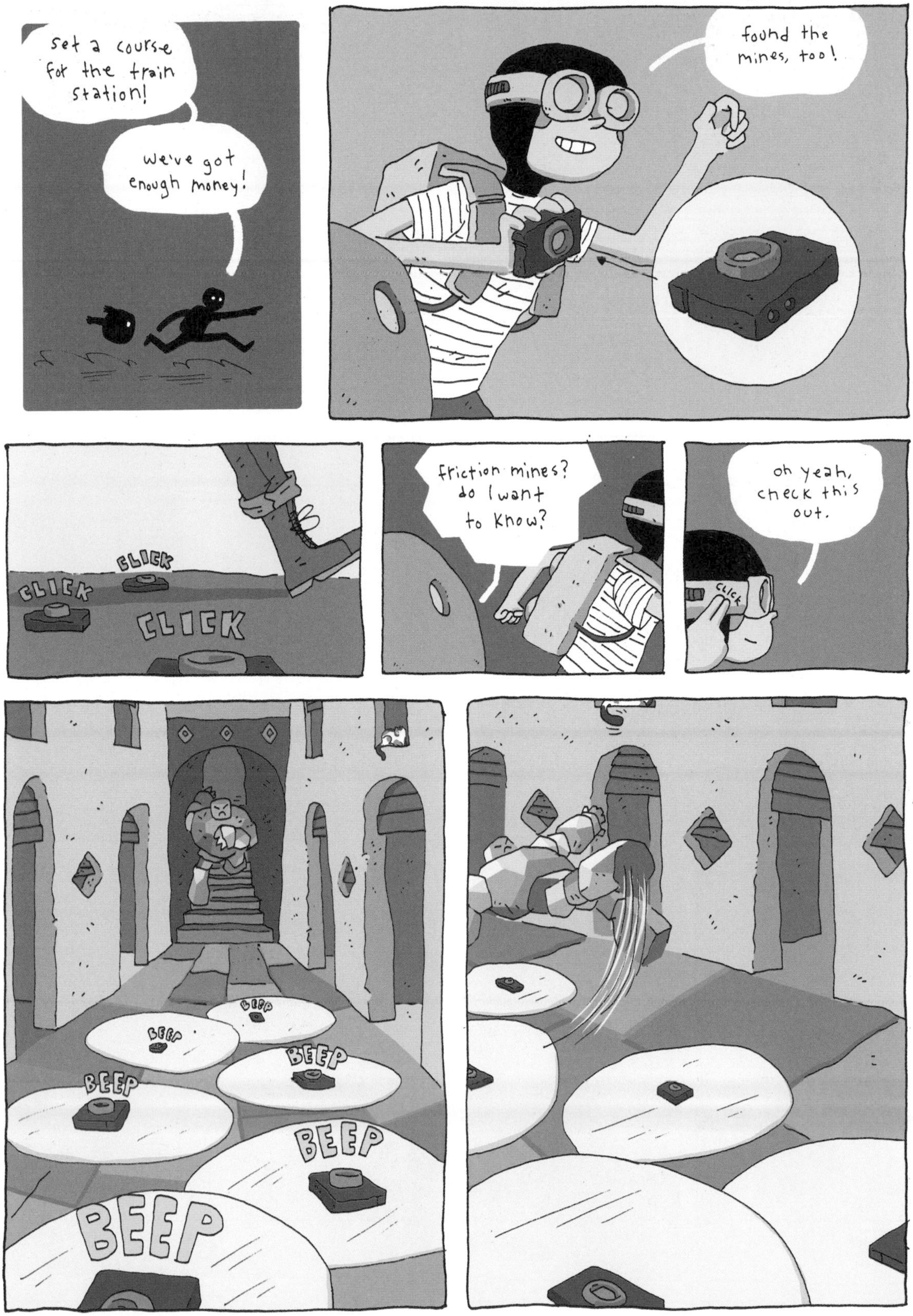
set a course for the train station!
we've got enough money!
found the mines, too!
CLICK
CLICK
CLICK
friction mines? do I want to know?
oh yeah, check this out.
CLICK
BEEP
BEEP
BEEP
BEEP
BEEP
BEEP

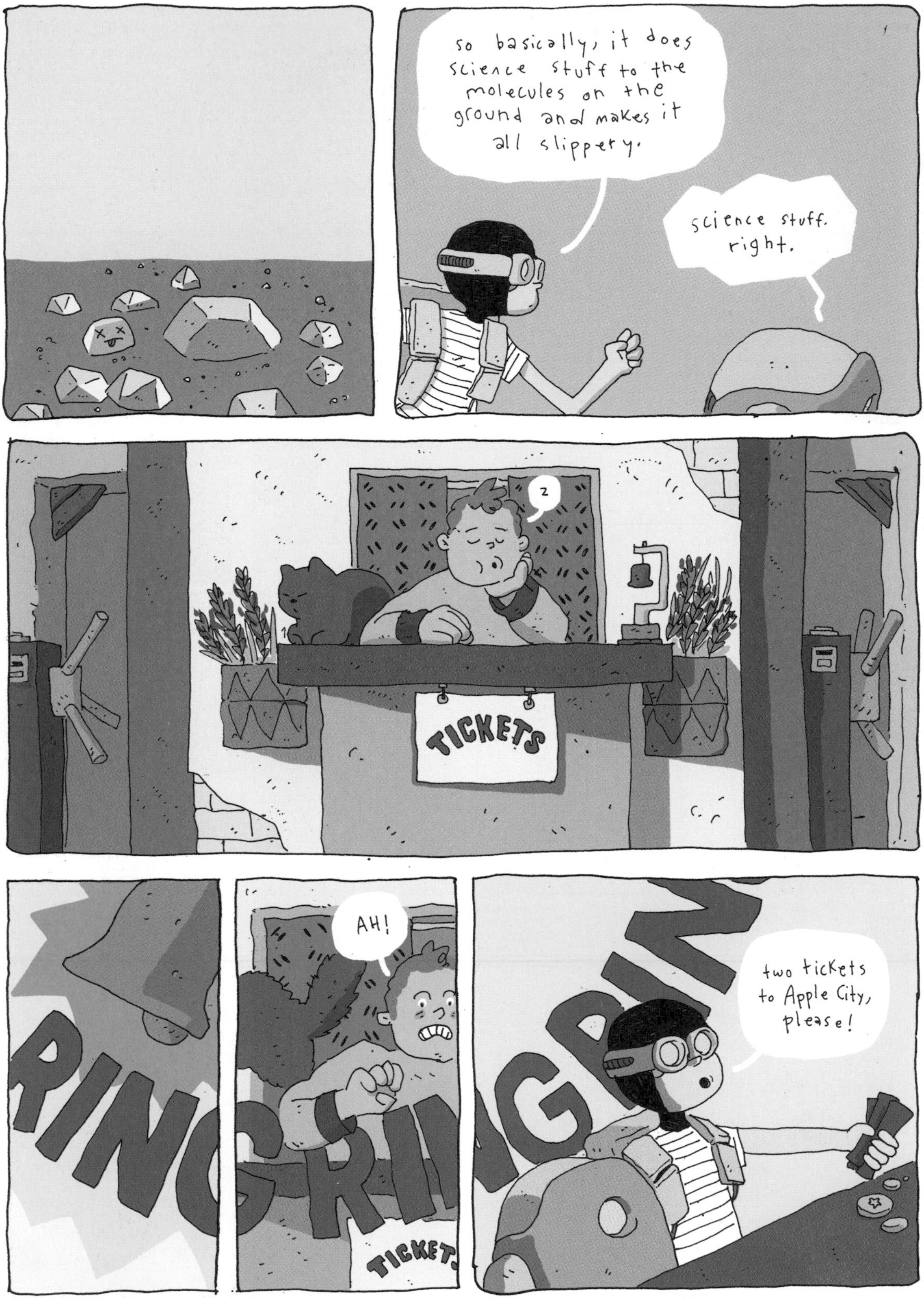
so basically, it does science stuff to the molecules on the ground and makes it all slippery.
science stuff. right.
z
TICKETS
RING
RING
AH!
TICKETS
two tickets to Apple City, please!

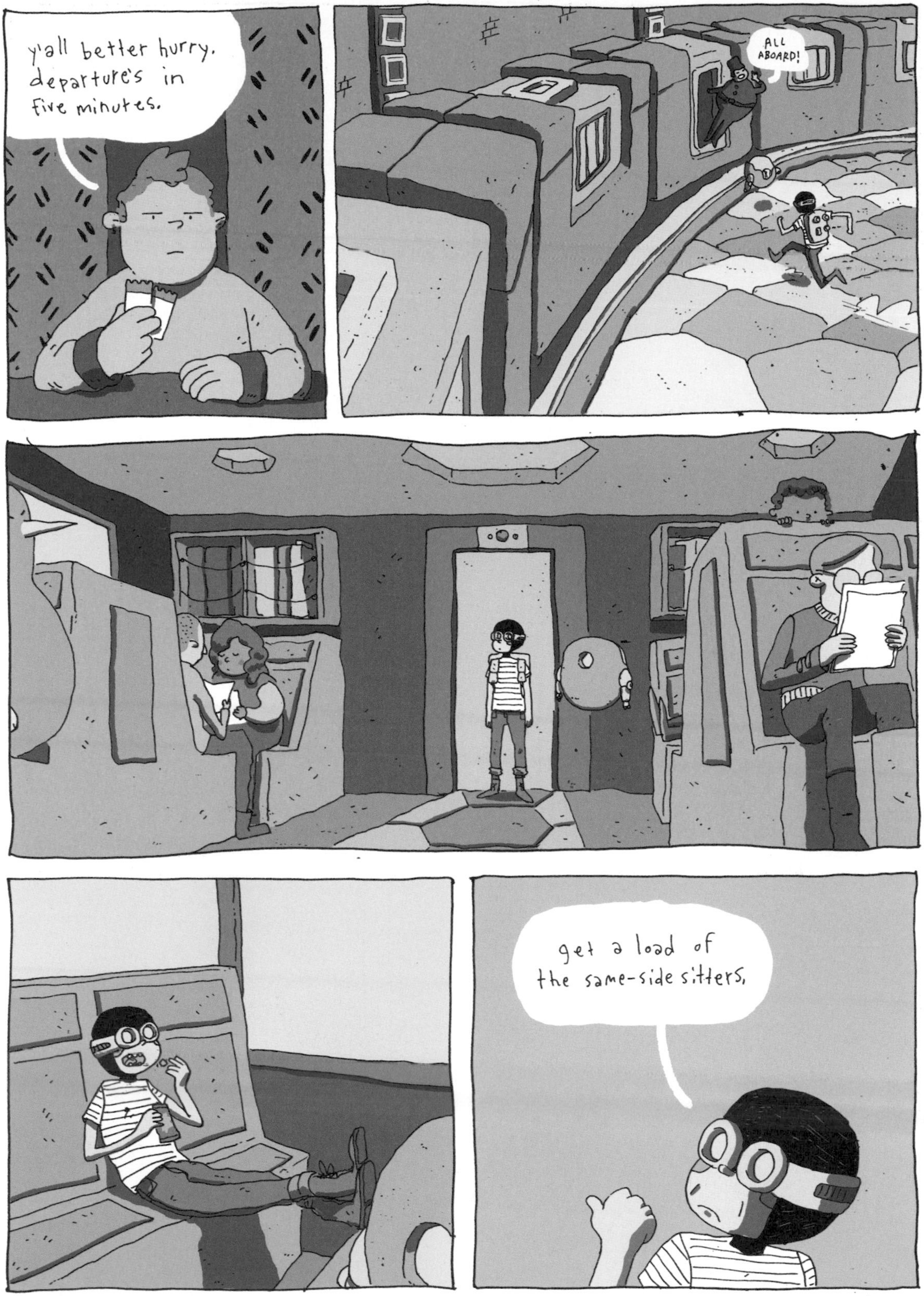
y'all better hurry. departure's in five minutes.
ALL ABOARD!
get a load of the same-side sitters.

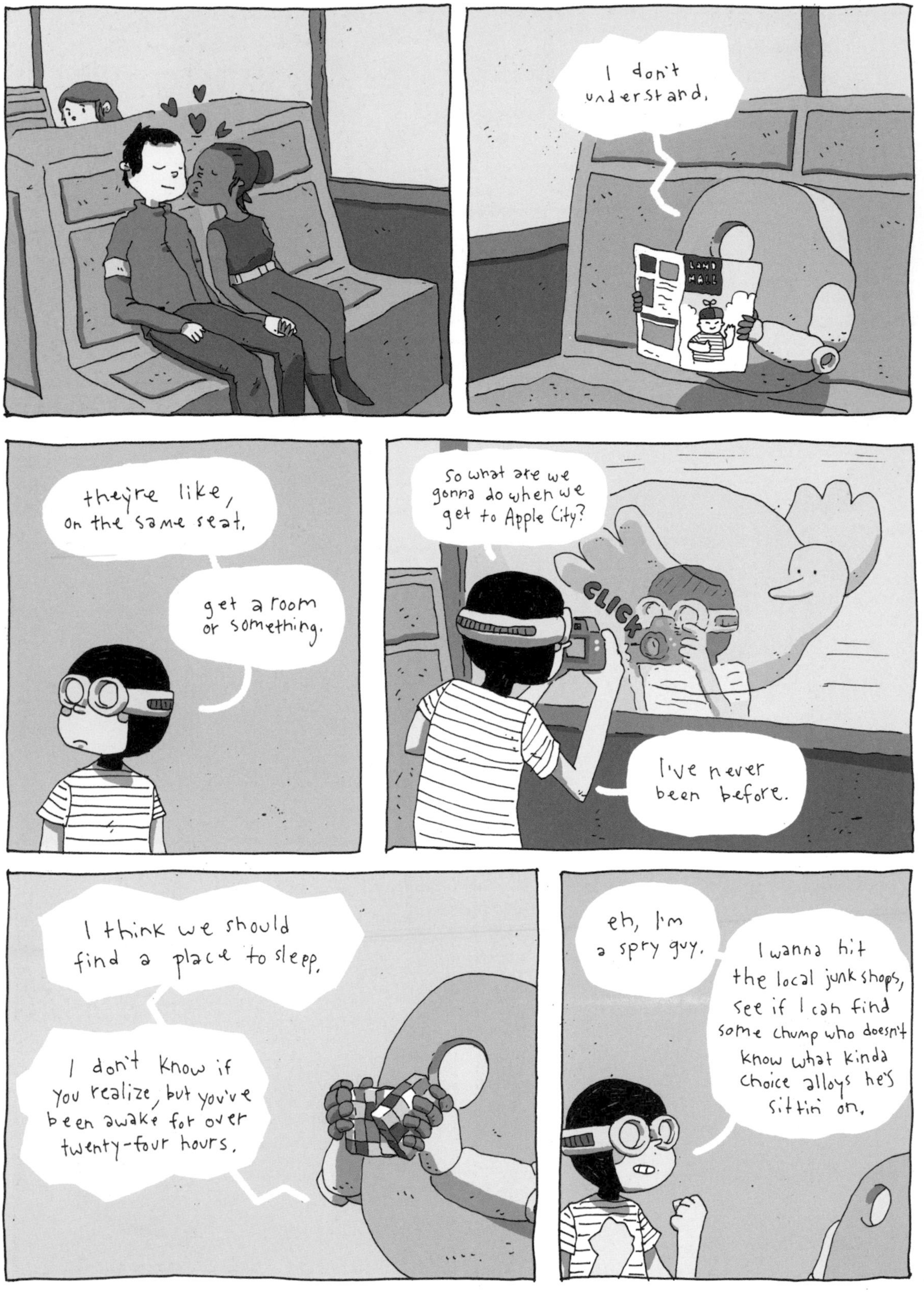

I don't understand,
LAND HALL
theyre like, on the same seat,
get a room or something.
So what are we gonna do when we get to Apple City?
CLICK
I've never been before.
I think we should find a place to slepp,
I don't know if you realize, but you've been awake for over twenty-four hours,
eh, I'm a spry guy,
I wanna hit the local junk shops, see if I can find some chump who doesn't know what kinda choice alloys he's sittin' on,

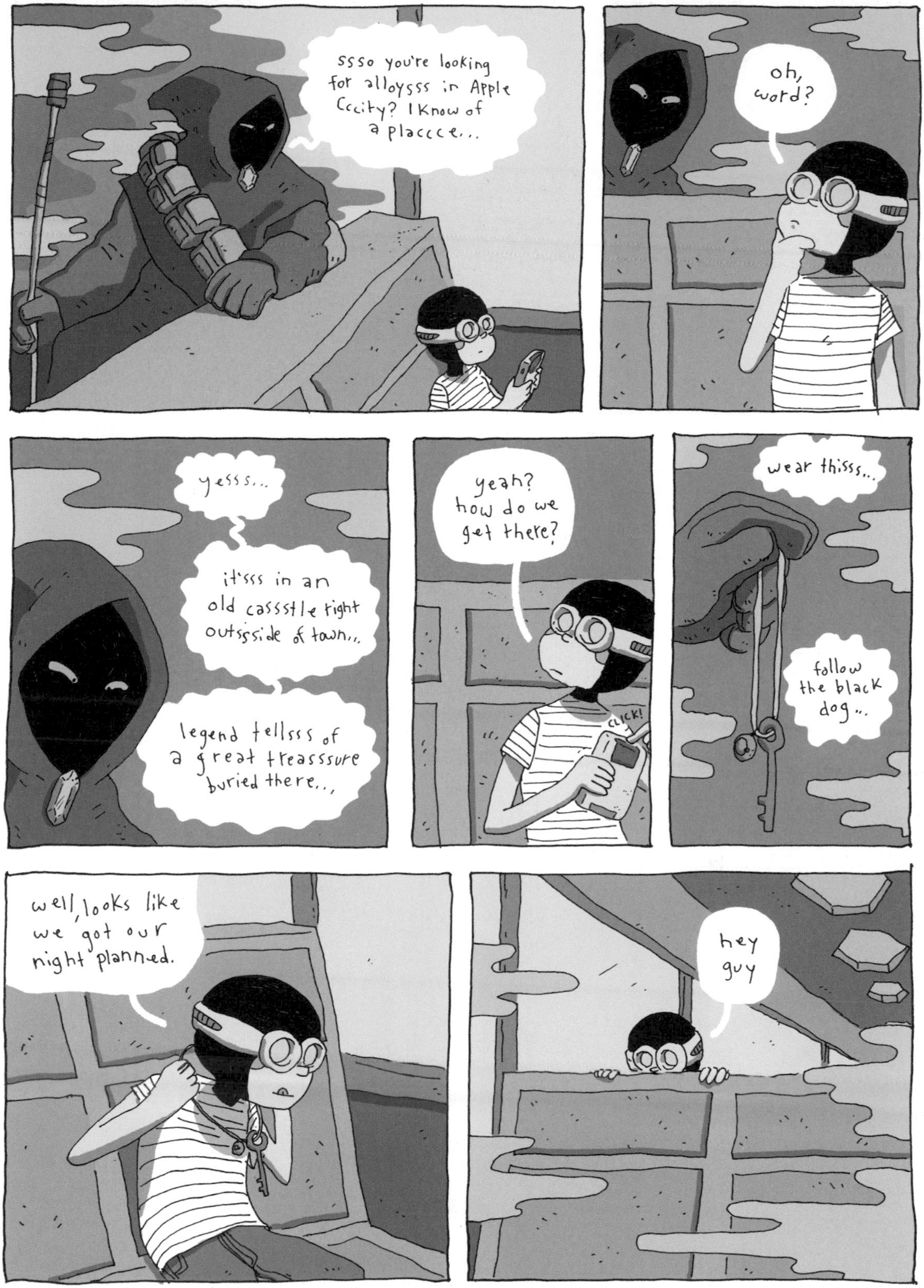
ssso you're looking for alloysss in Apple Cccity? I know of a placcce...
oh, word?
yesss...
it'sss in an old cassstle right outsssside of town...
legend tellsss of a great treasssure buried there...
yeah? how do we get there?
CLICK!
wear thisss...
follow the black dog...
well, looks like we got our night planned.
hey guy

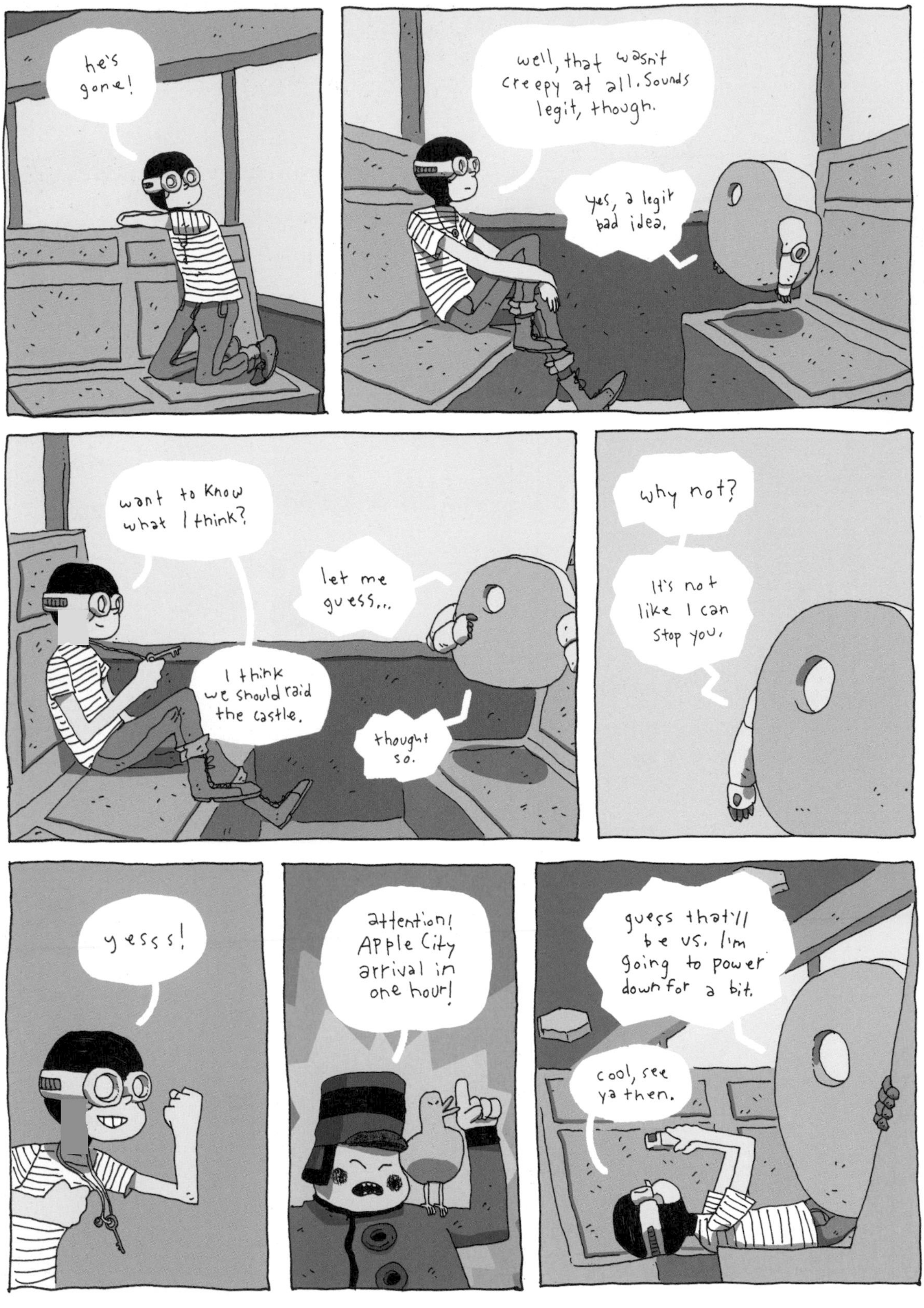
he's gone!
well, that wasn't creepy at all. Sounds legit, though.
yes, a legit bad idea.
want to know what I think?
let me guess...
I think we should raid the castle.
thought so.
why not?
It's not like I can stop you.
yesss!
attention! Apple City arrival in one hour!
guess that'll be us. I'm going to power down for a bit.
cool, see ya then.

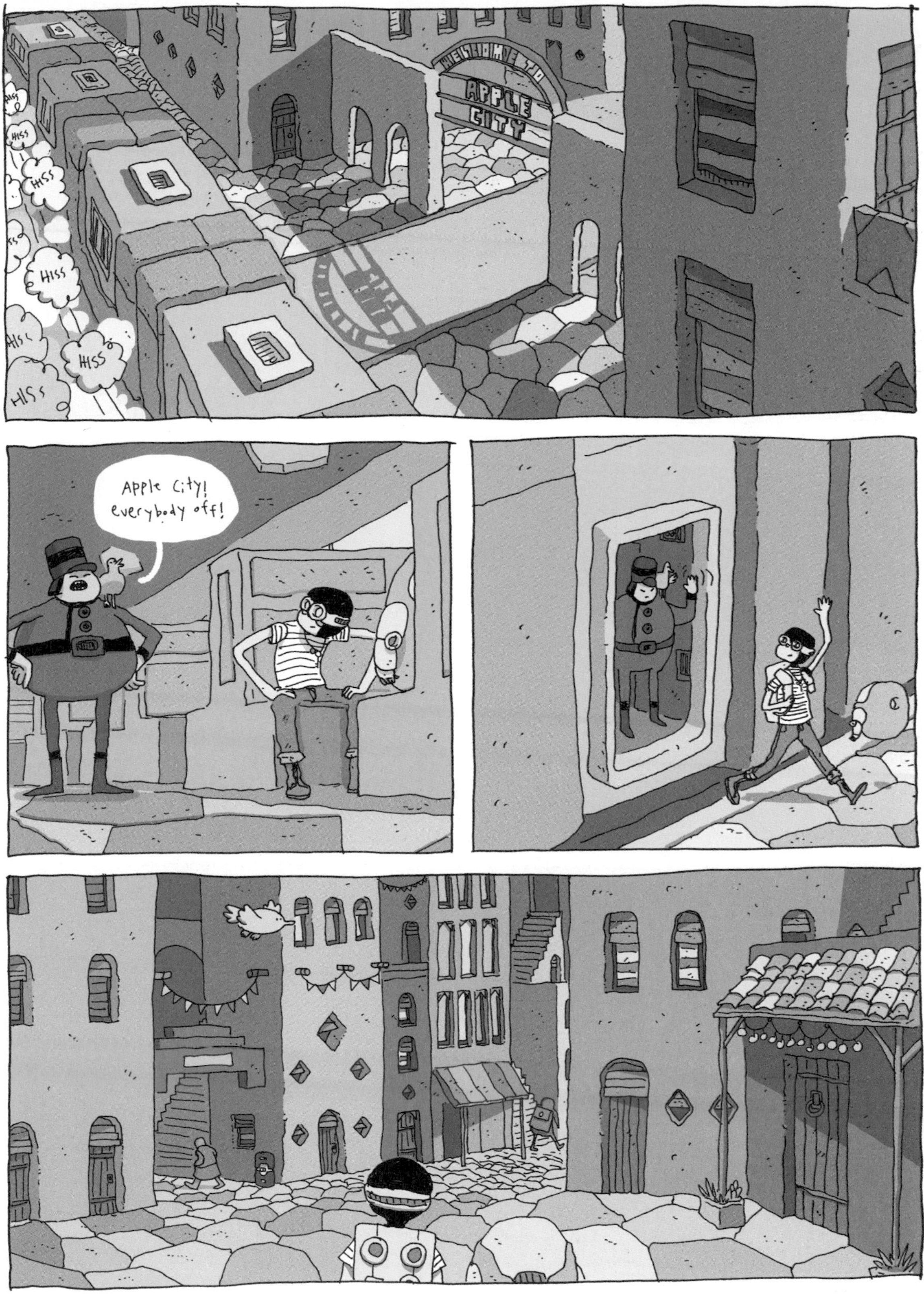
WELCOME TO
APPLE CITY
HISS
HISS
HISS
HISS
HISS
HISS
Apple City! everybody off!

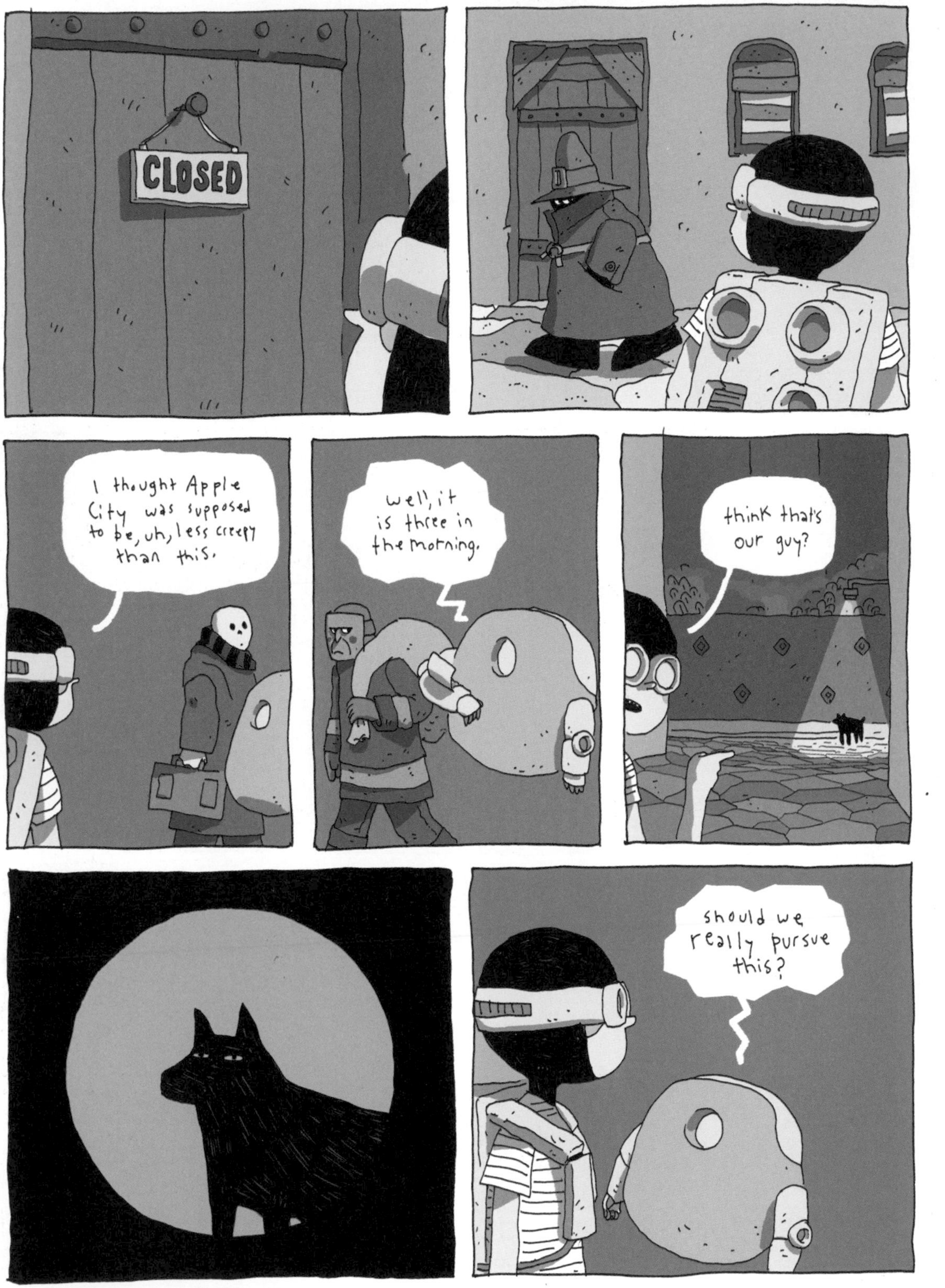
CLOSED
I thought Apple City was supposed to be, uh, less creepy than this.
well, it is three in the morning.
think that's our guy?
should we really pursue this?

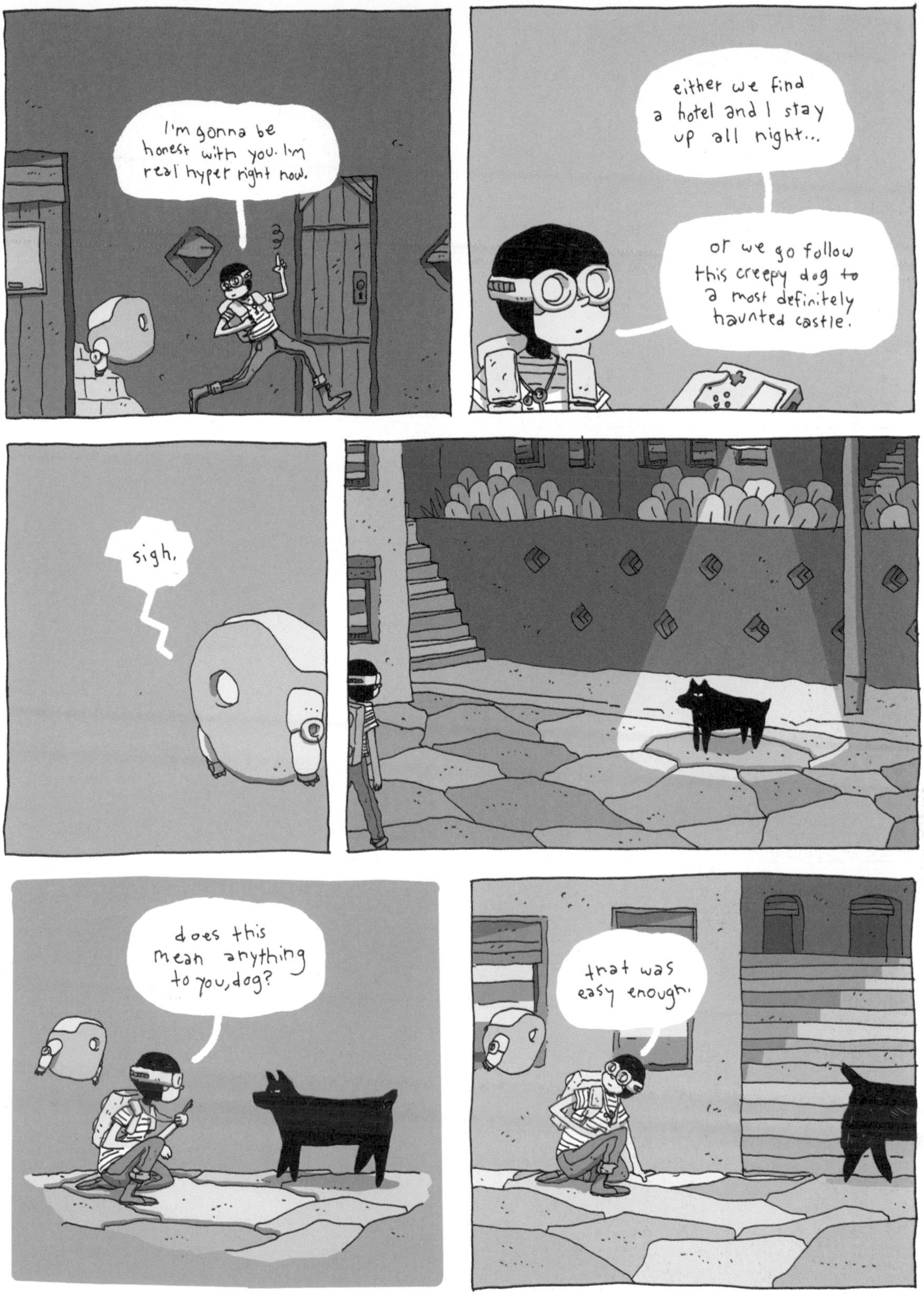
I'm gonna be honest with you. I'm real hyper right now.
either we find a hotel and I stay up all night...
or we go follow this creepy dog to a most definitely haunted castle.
sigh.
does this mean anything to you, dog?
that was easy enough.

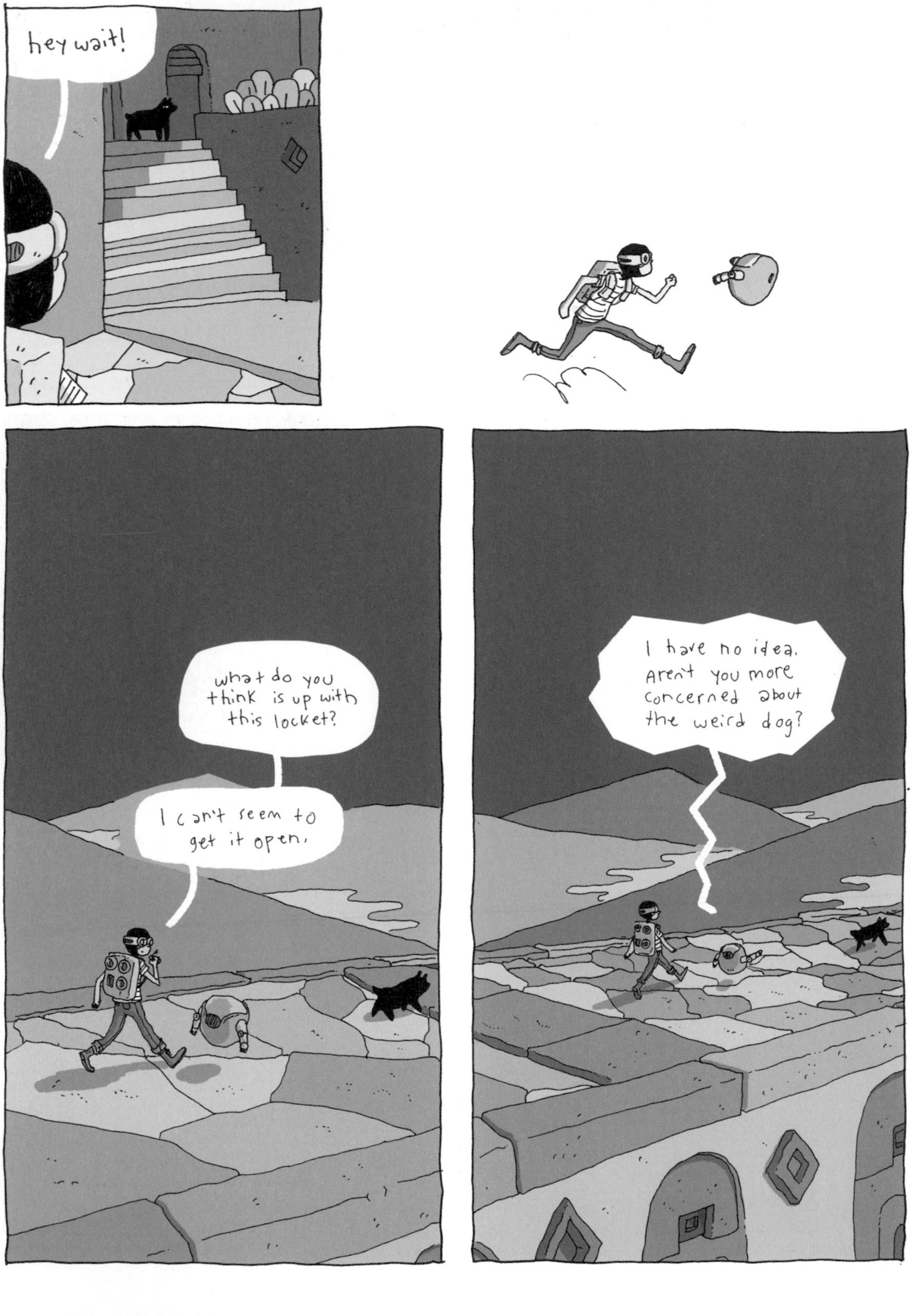
hey wait!
what do you think is up with this locket?
I can't seem to get it open.
I have no idea. Aren't you more concerned about the weird dog?

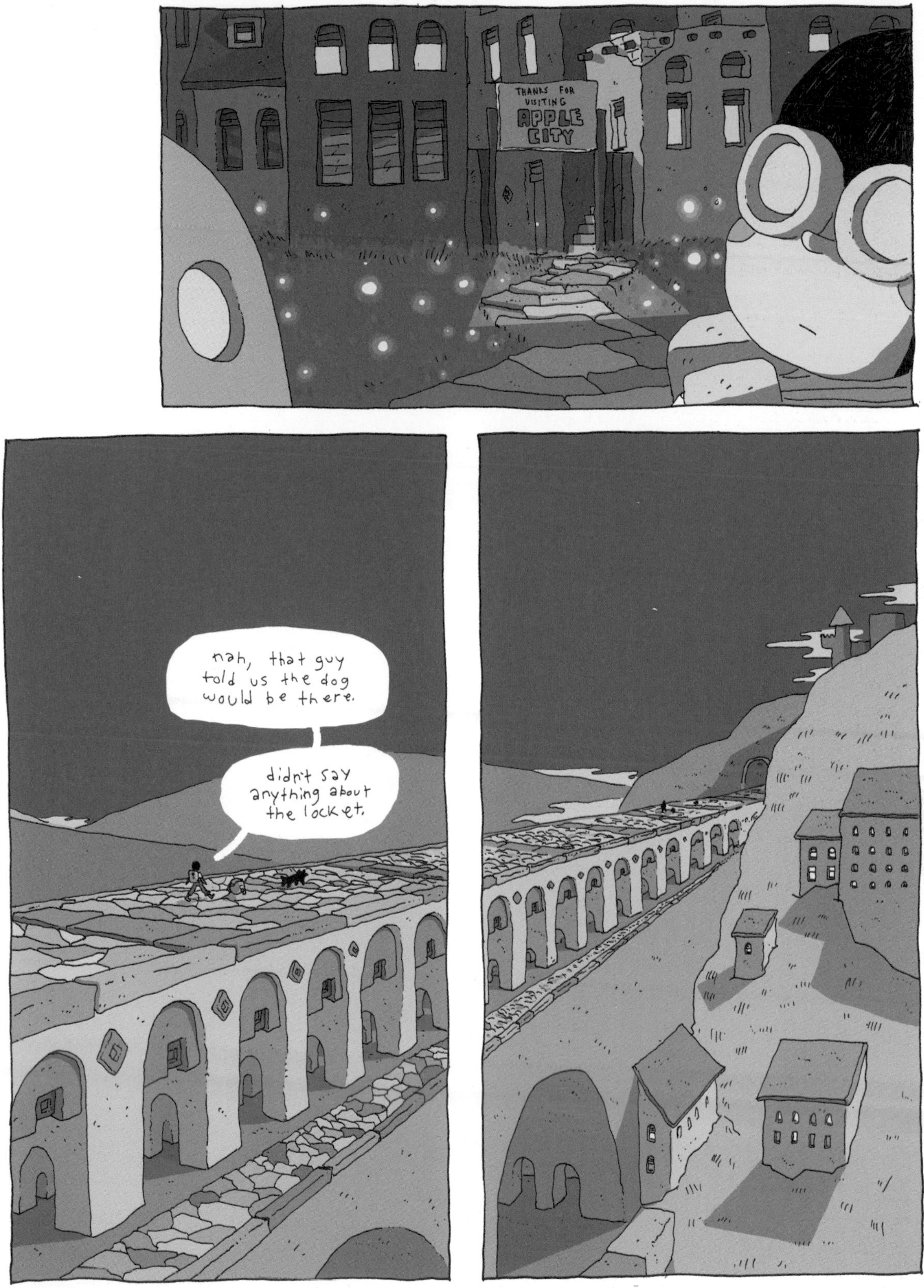
THANKS FOR VISITING APPLE CITY
nah, that guy told us the dog would be there.
didn't say anything about the locket.

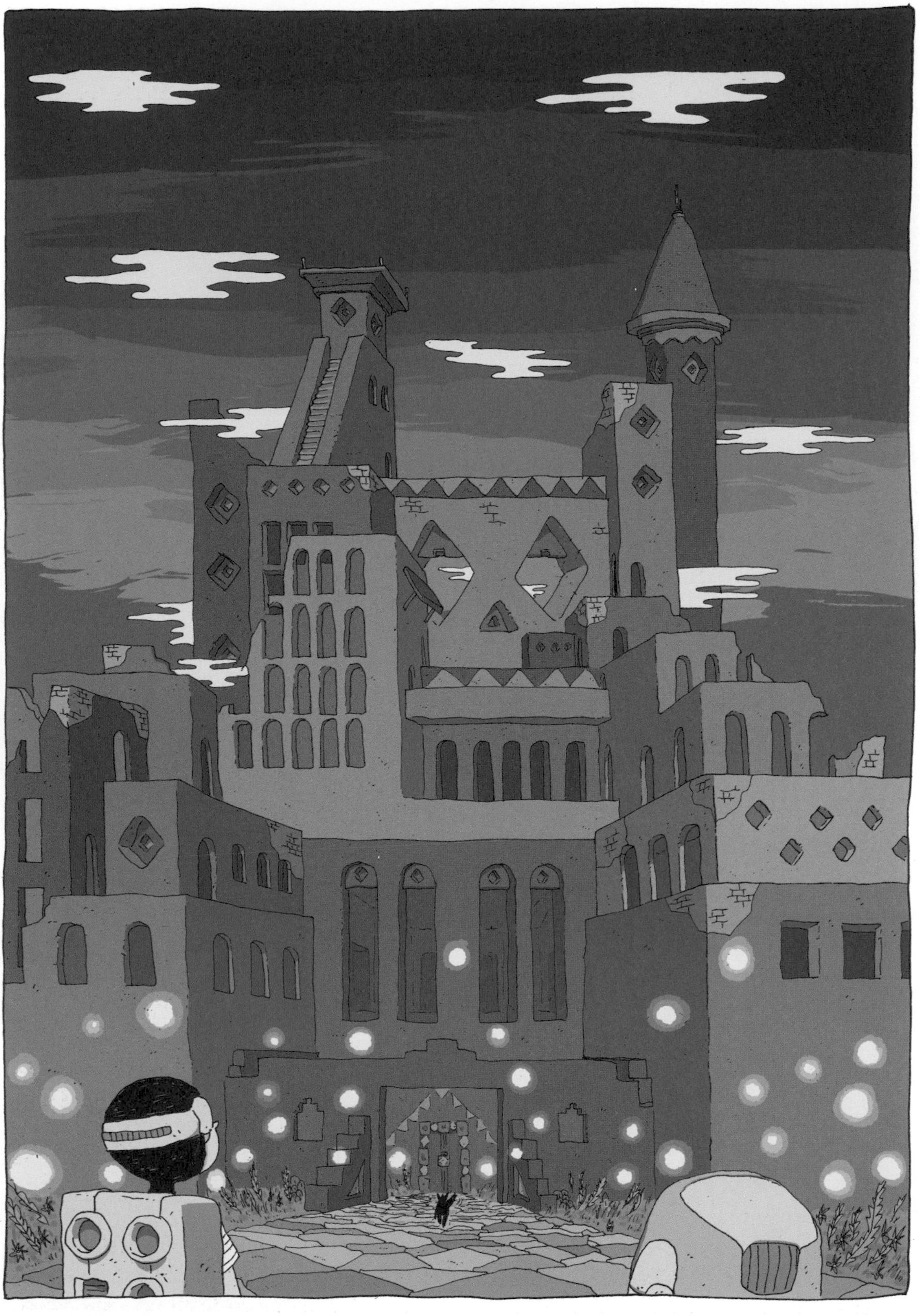

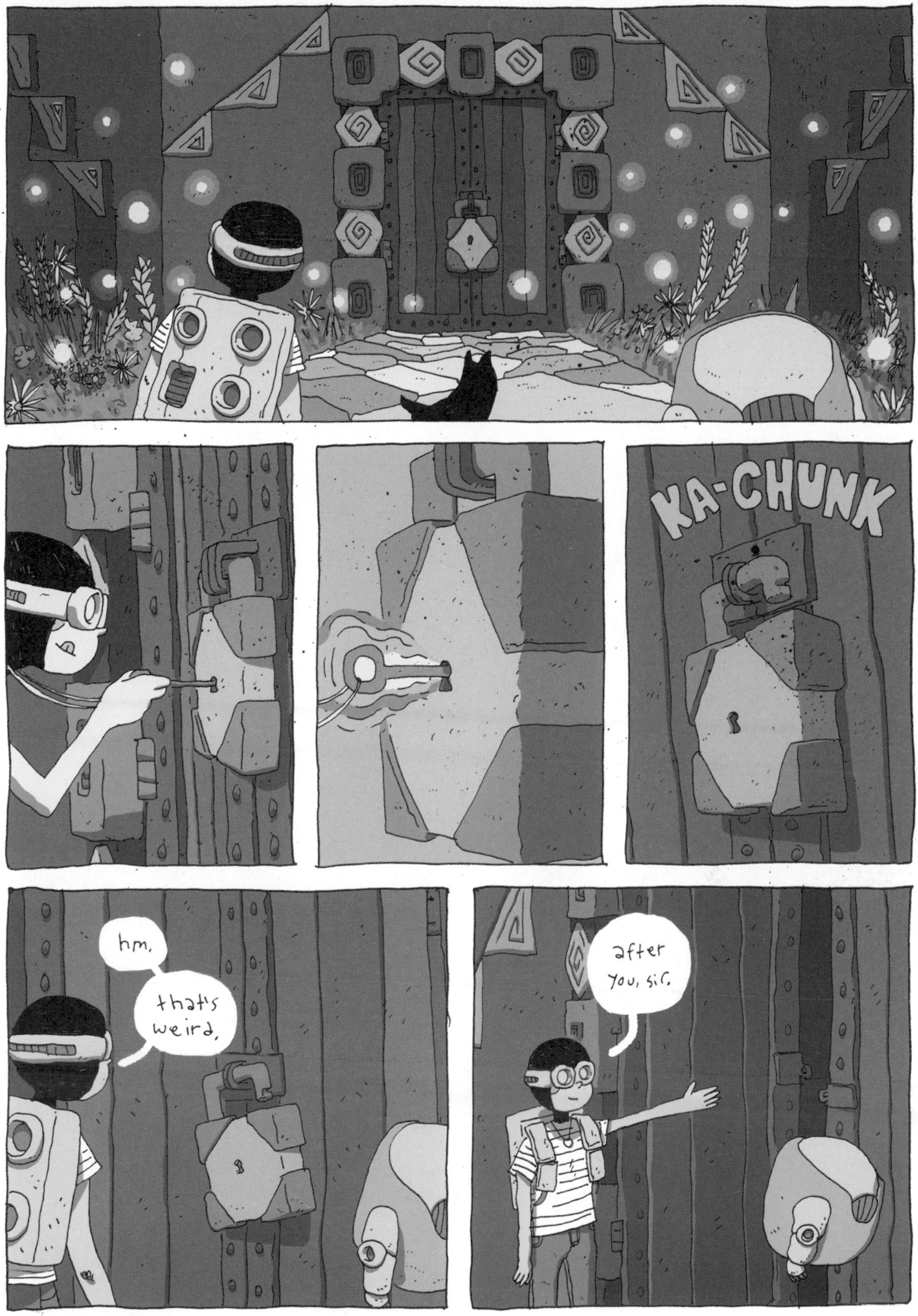
KA-CHUNK
hm.
that's weird.
after you, sir.

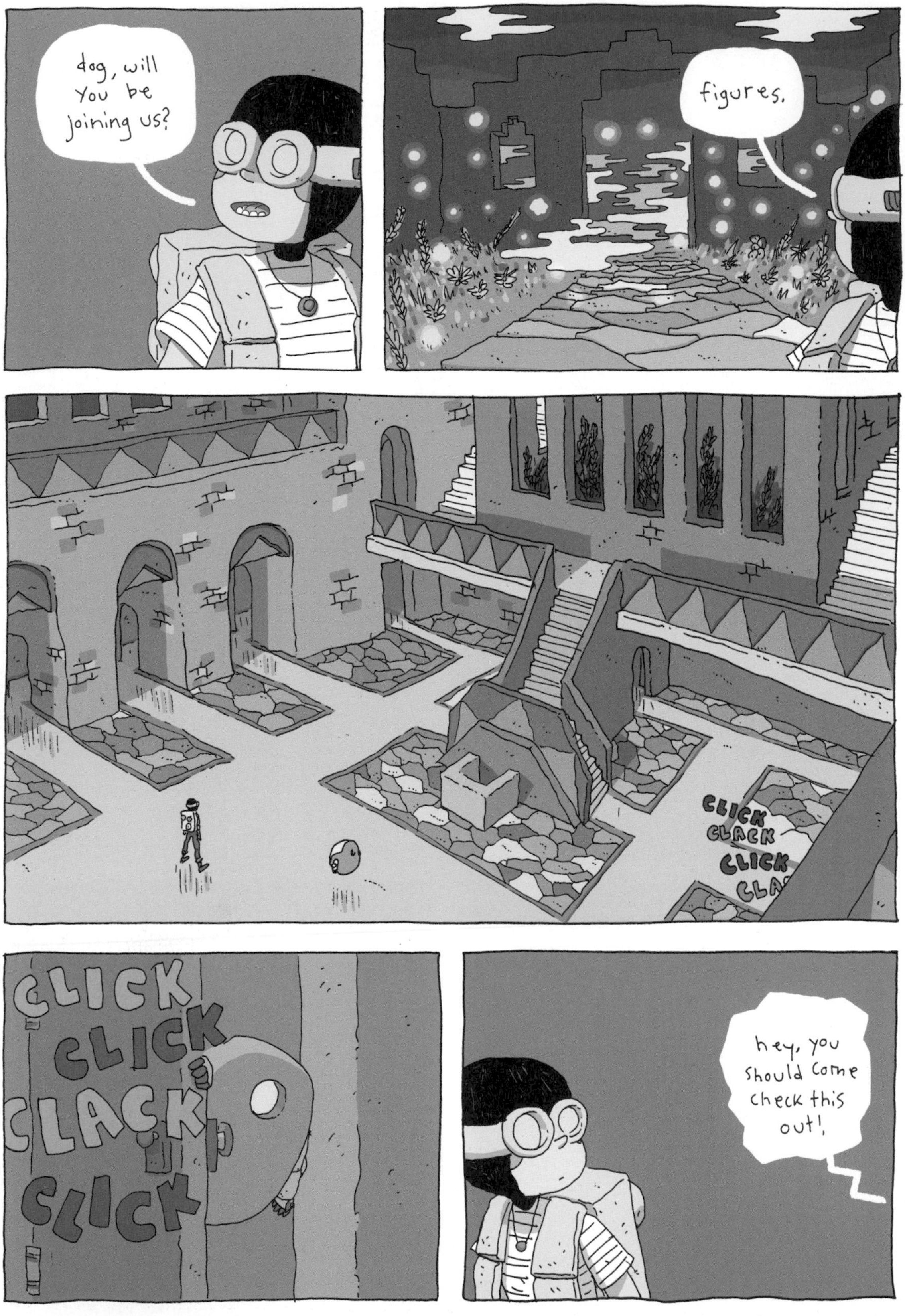
dog, will you be joining us?
figures.
CLICK CLACK CLICK CLA
CLICK CLICK CLACK CLICK
hey, you should come check this out!

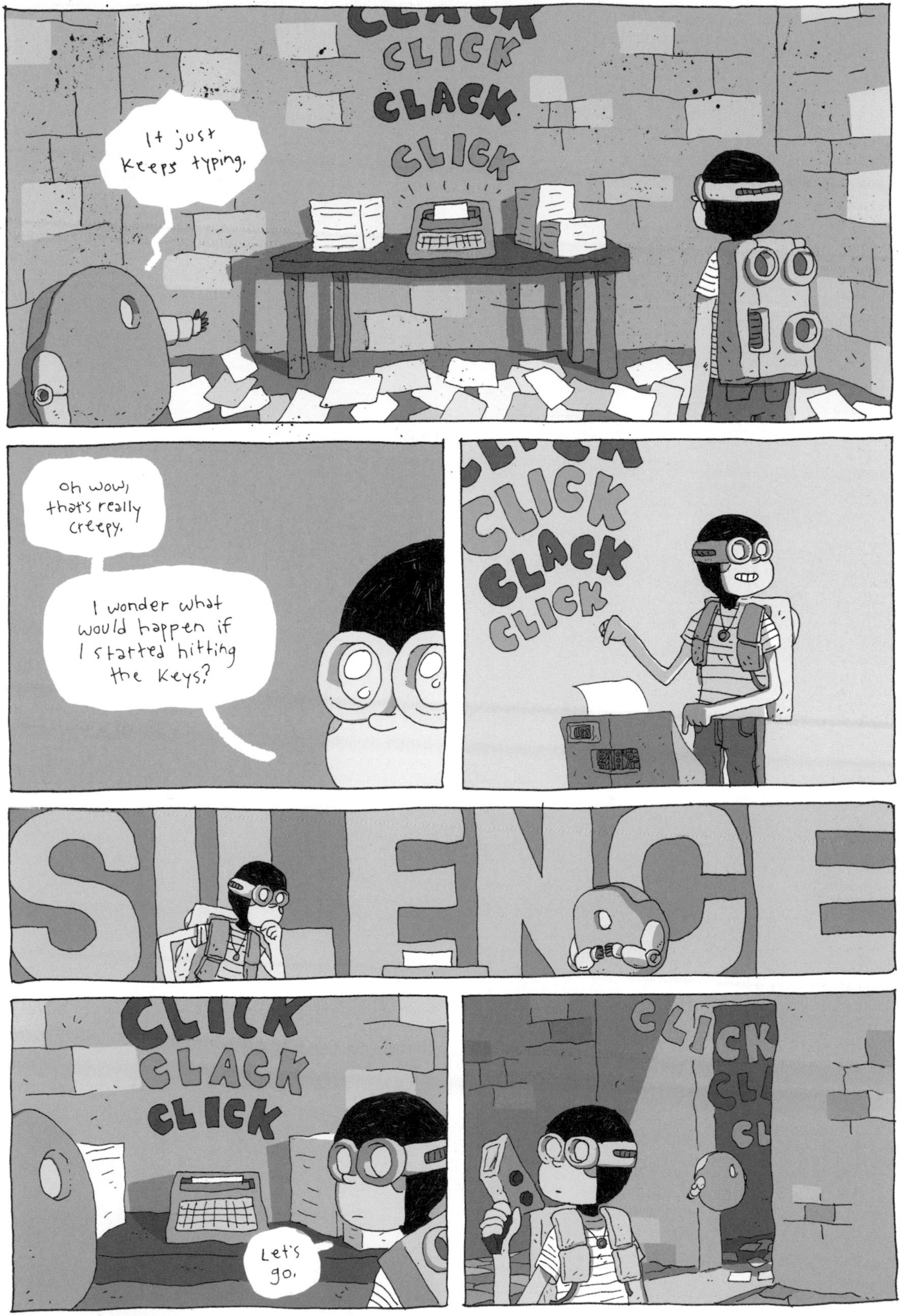
CLICK
CLACK
CLICK
It just keeps typing.
Oh wow, that's really creepy.
I wonder what would happen if I started hitting the keys?
CLICK
CLACK
CLICK
SILENCE
CLICK
CLACK
CLICK
Let's go.
CLICK

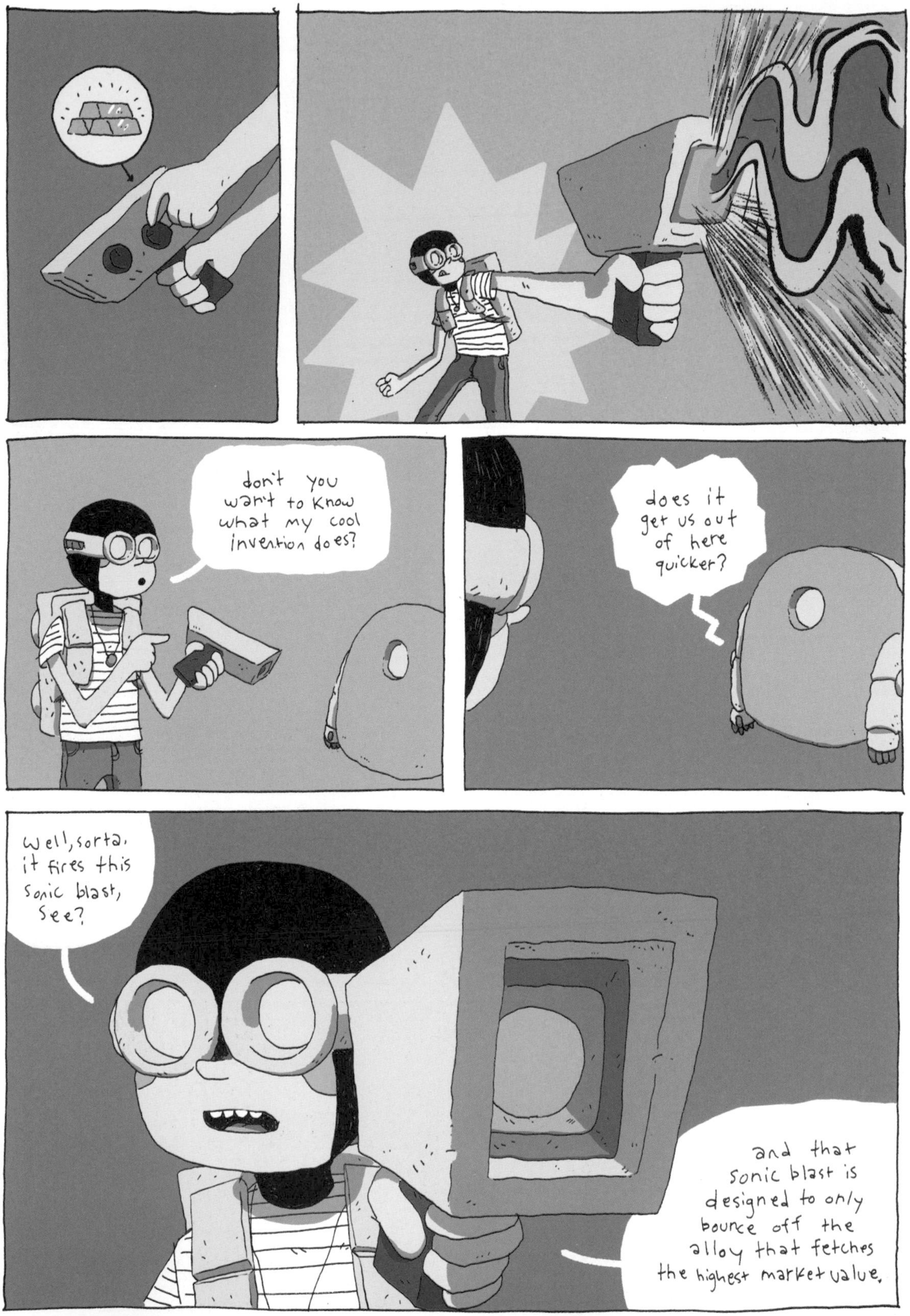
don't you want to know what my cool invention does?
does it get us out of here quicker?
well, sorta. it fires this sonic blast, see?
and that sonic blast is designed to only bounce off the alloy that fetches the highest market value.

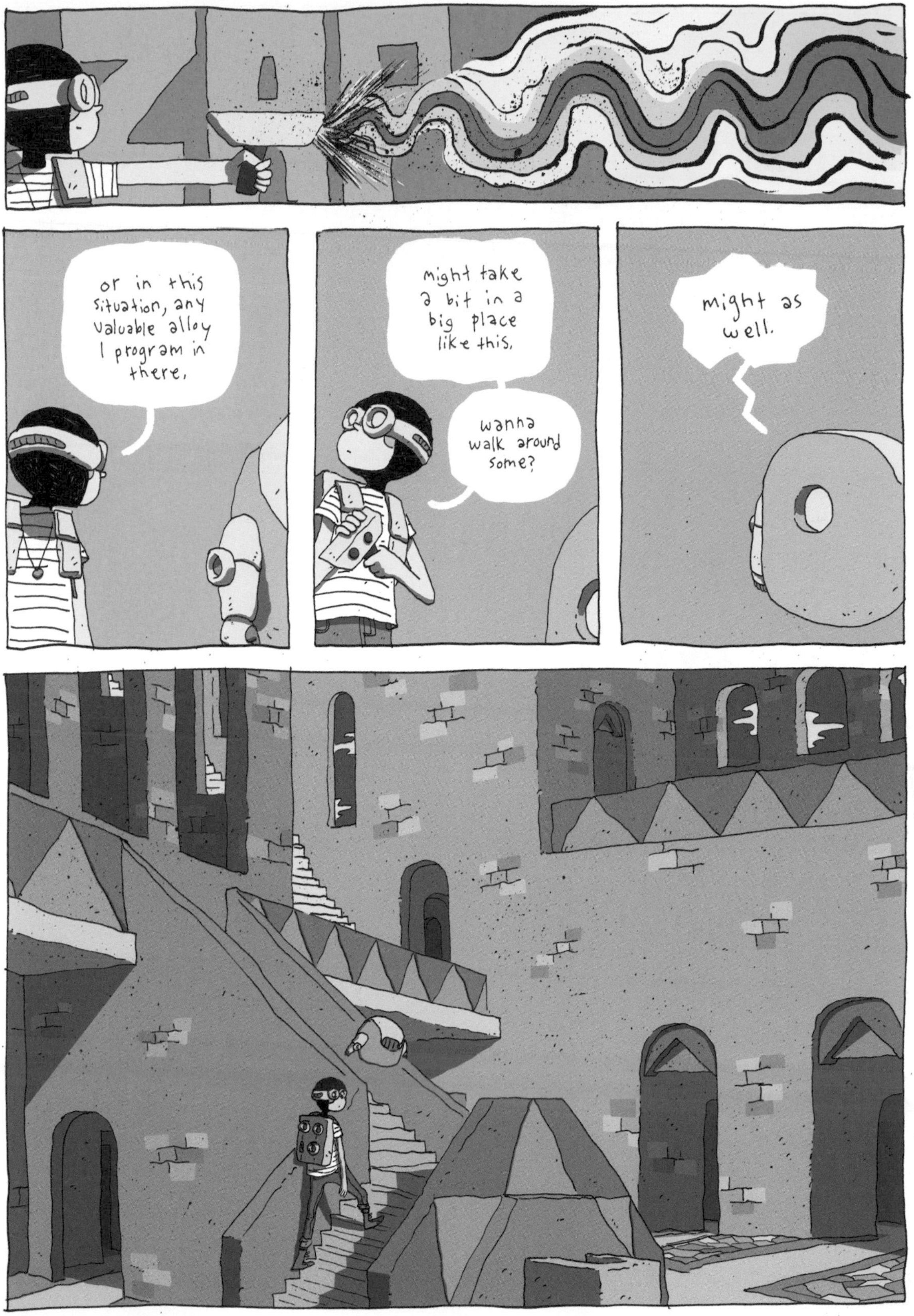
or in this situation, any valuable alloy I program in there.
might take a bit in a big place like this.
wanna walk around some?
might as well.

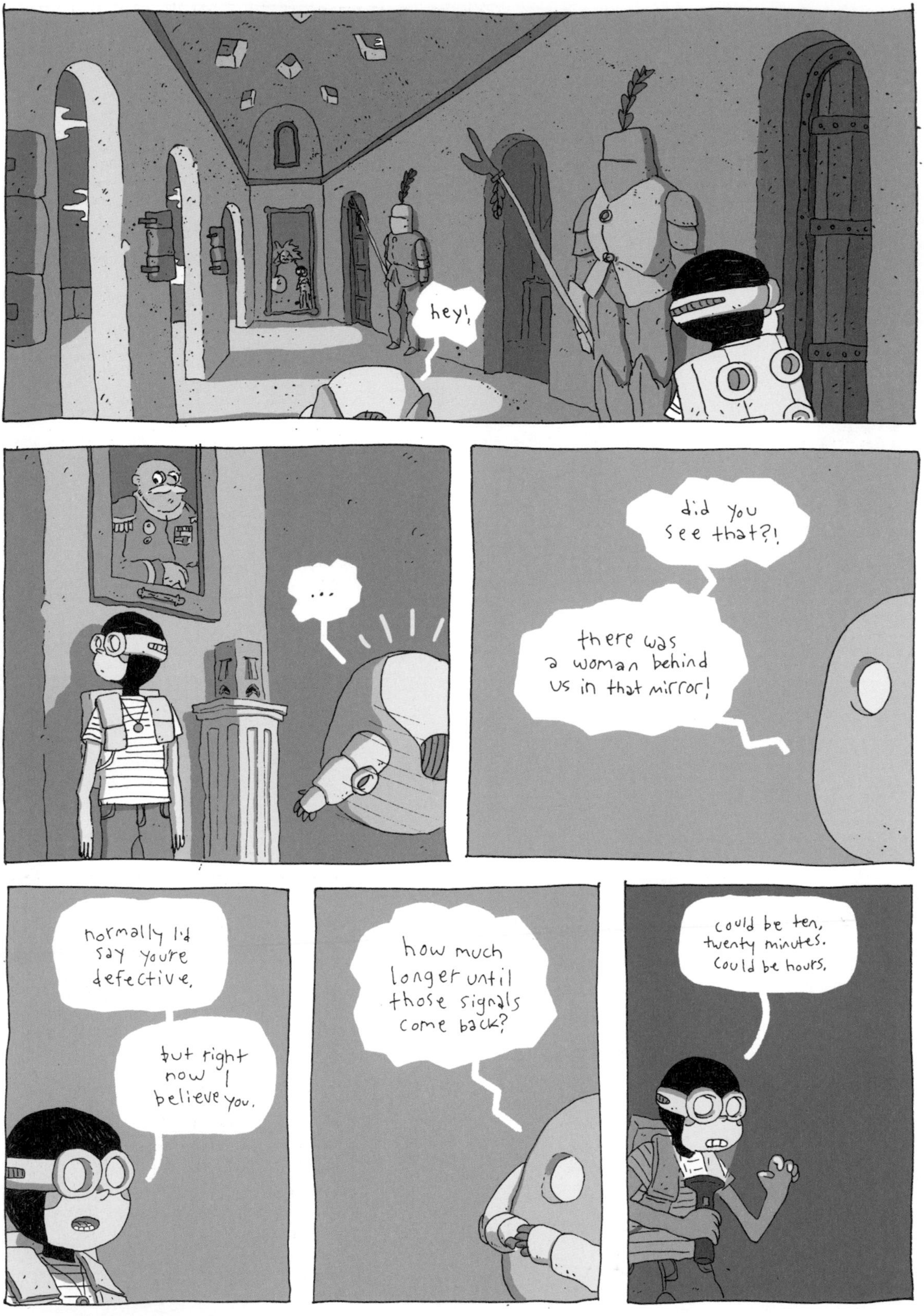
hey!
...
did you see that?!
there was a woman behind us in that mirror!
normally I'd say you're defective.
but right now I believe you.
how much longer until those signals come back?
could be ten, twenty minutes. could be hours.

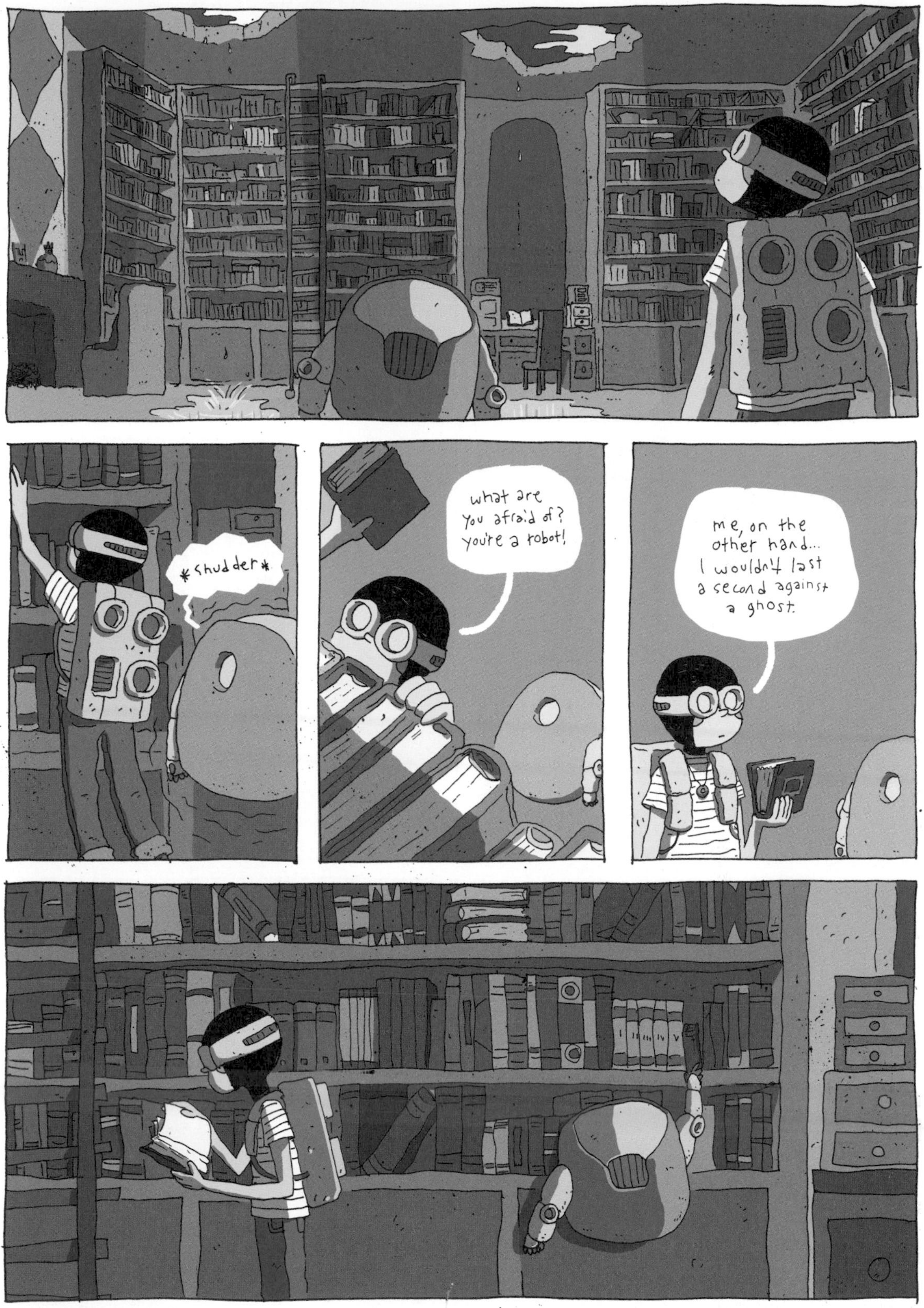
shudder
what are you afraid of? you're a robot!
me, on the other hand... I wouldn't last a second against a ghost.

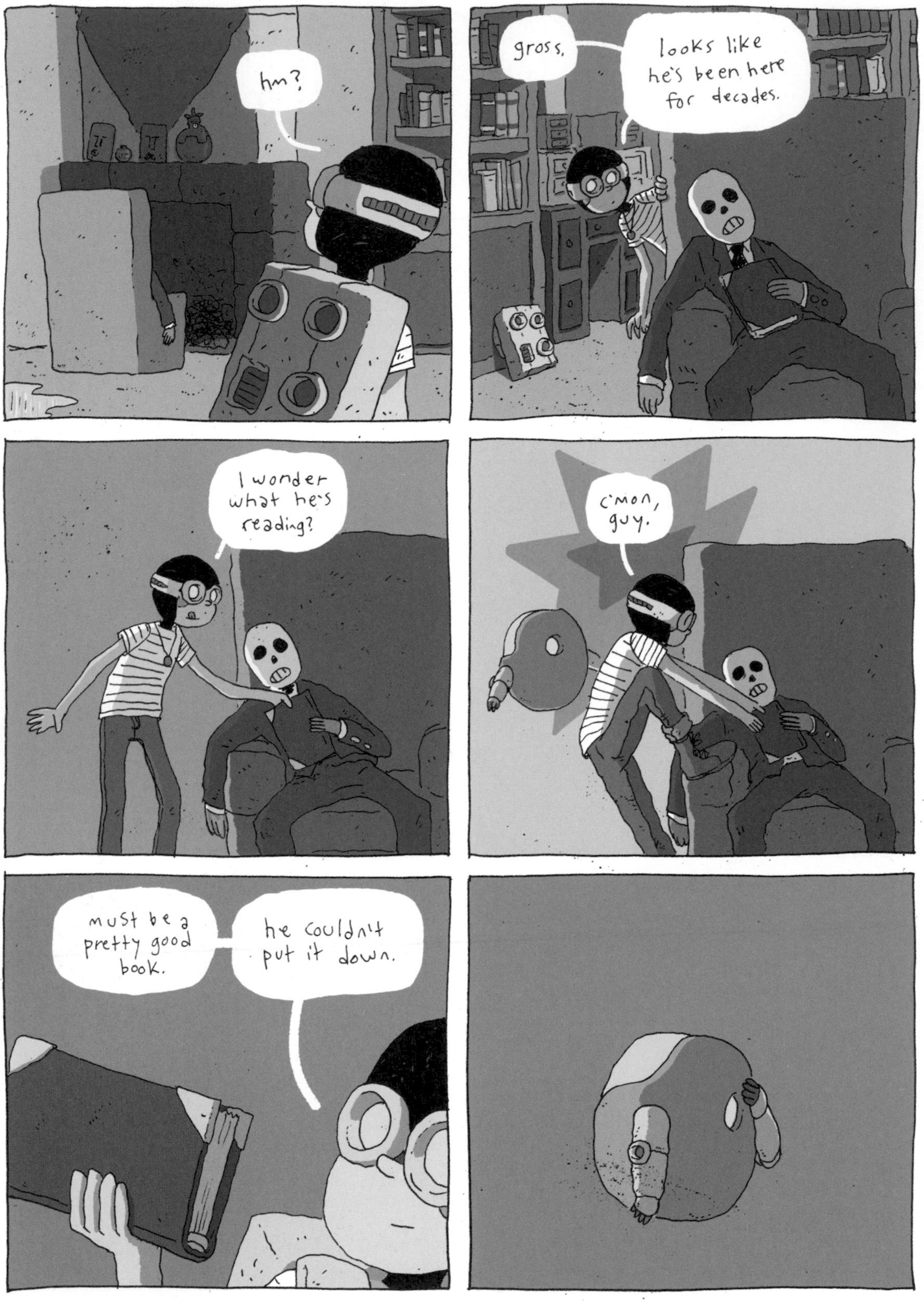
hm?
gross.
looks like he's been here for decades.
I wonder what he's reading?
c'mon, guy.
must be a pretty good book.
he couldn't put it down.

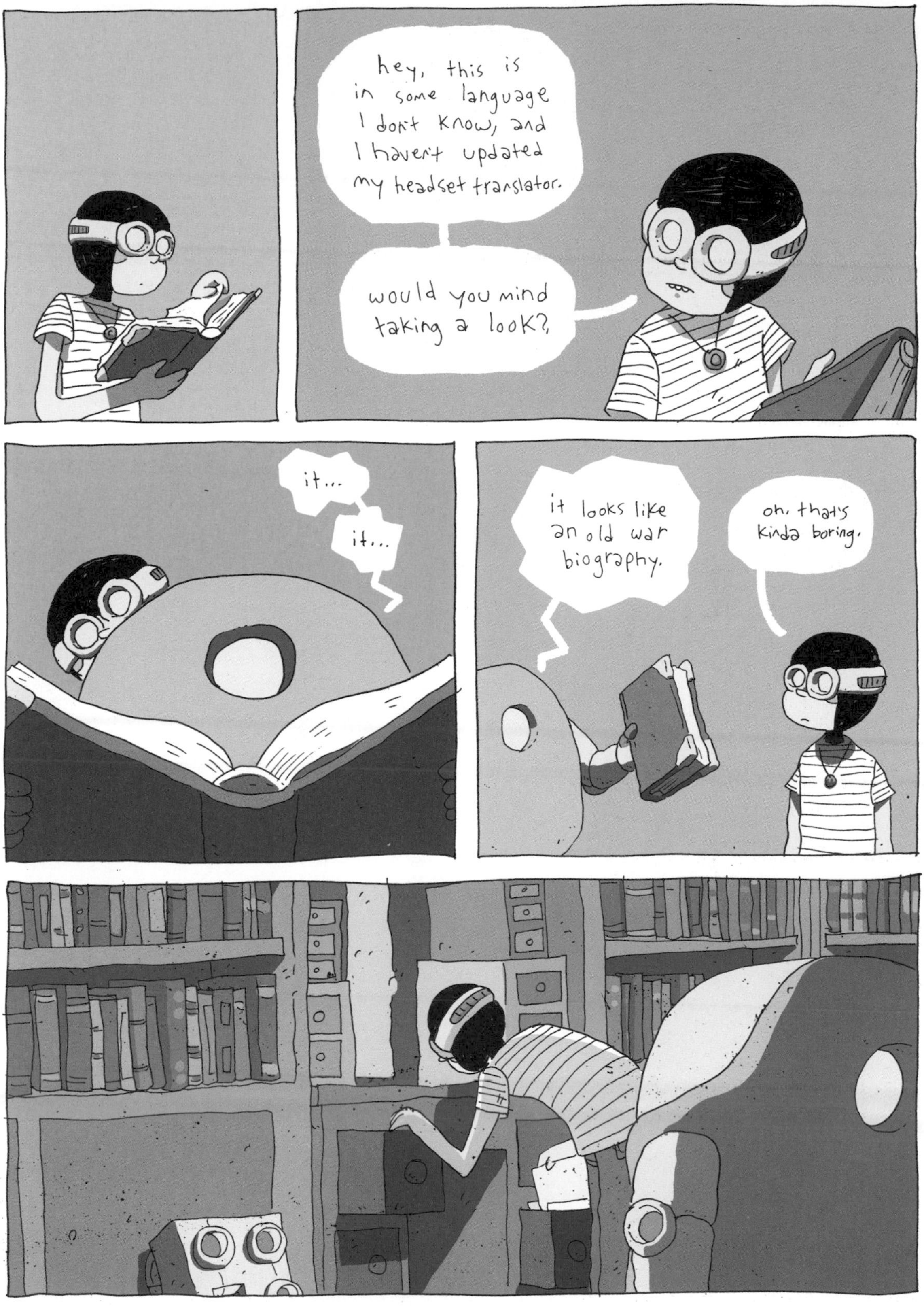

hey, this is in some language I don't know, and I haven't updated my headset translator.
would you mind taking a look?
it...
it...
it looks like an old war biography.
oh, that's kinda boring.

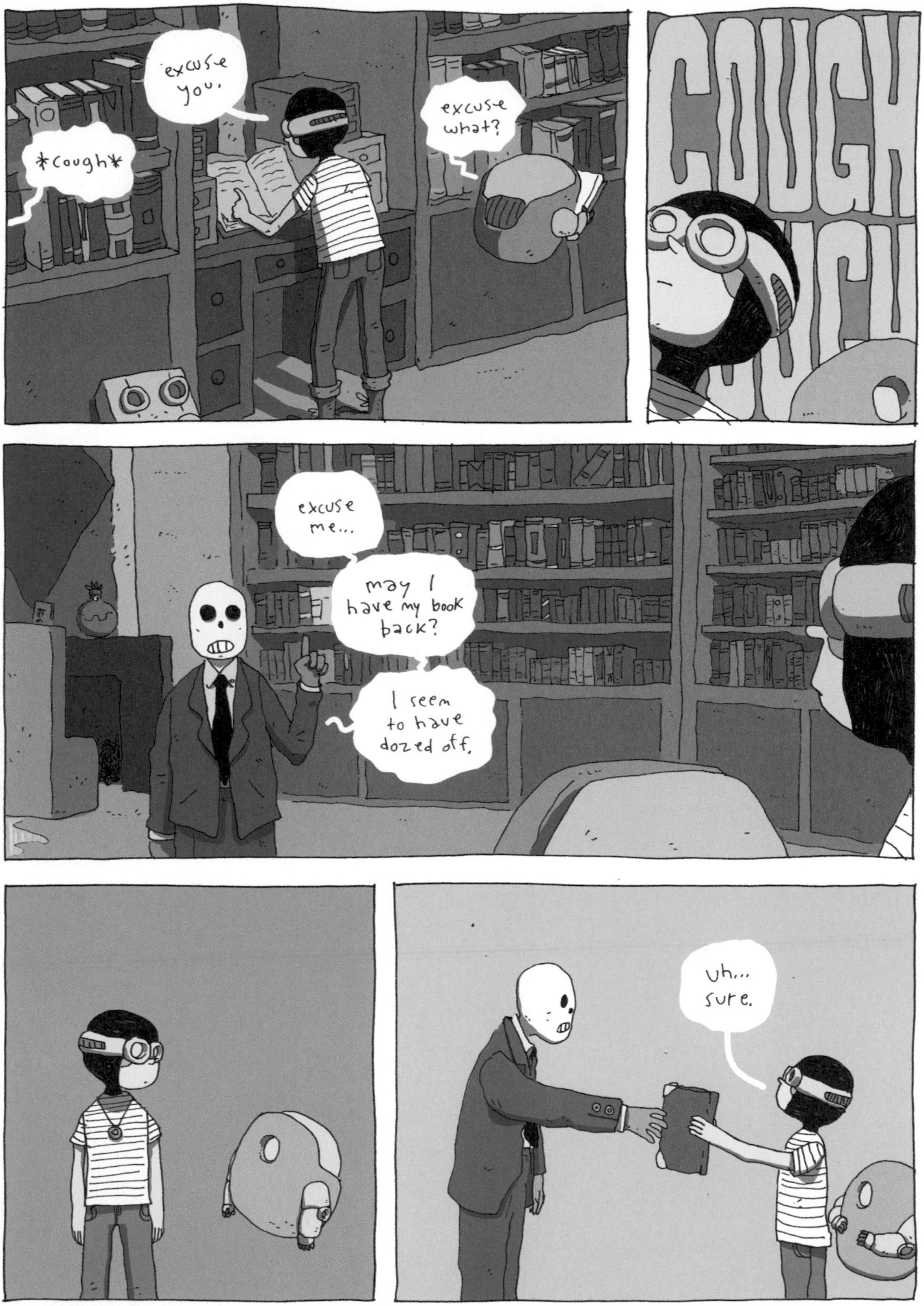
cough
excuse you.
excuse what?
COUGH COUGH
excuse me...
may I have my book back?
I seem to have dozed off.
uh... sure.

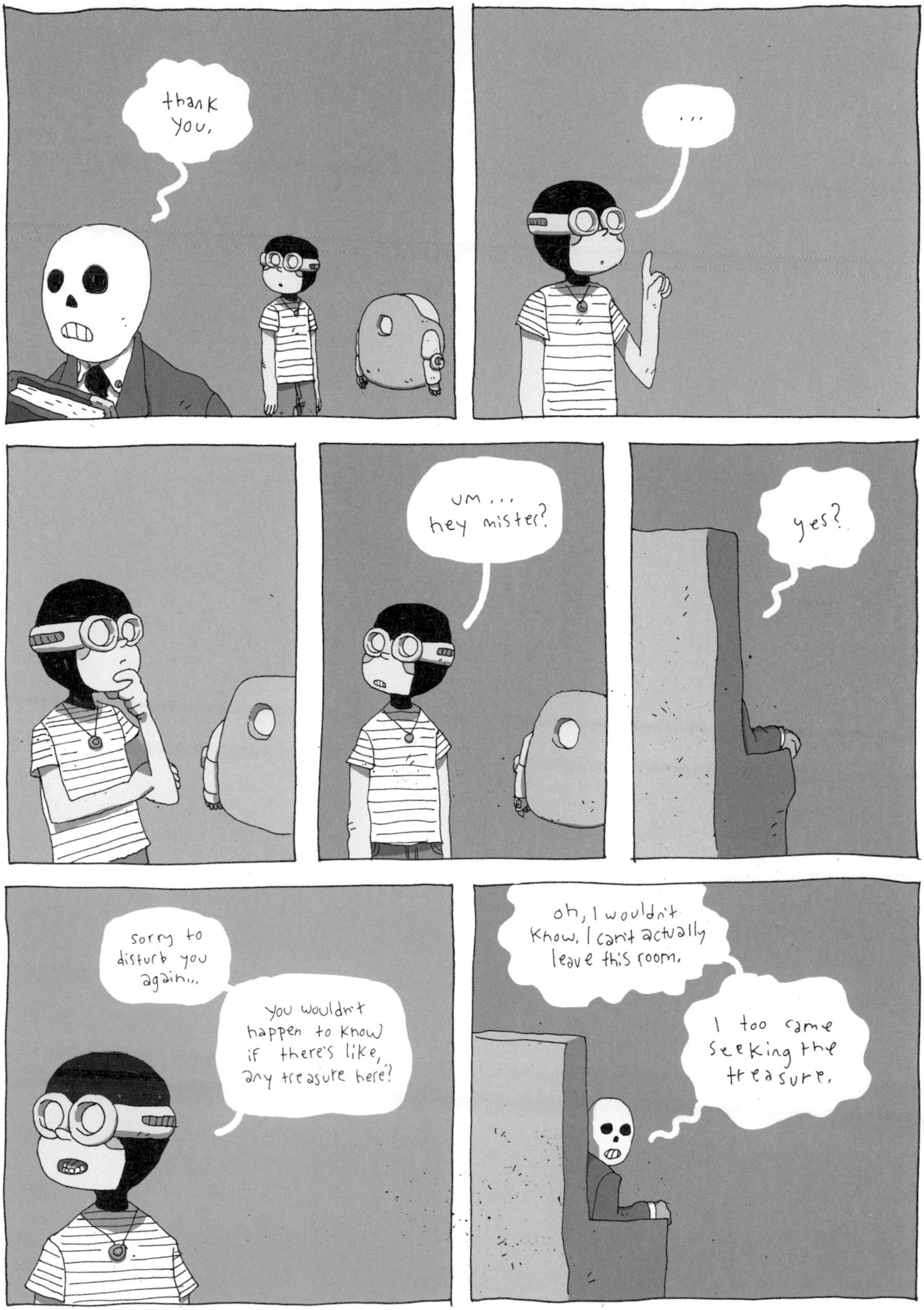
thank you.
...
um... hey mister?
yes?
sorry to disturb you again...
you wouldn't happen to know if there's like, any treasure here?
oh, I wouldn't know. I can't actually leave this room.
I too came seeking the treasure.

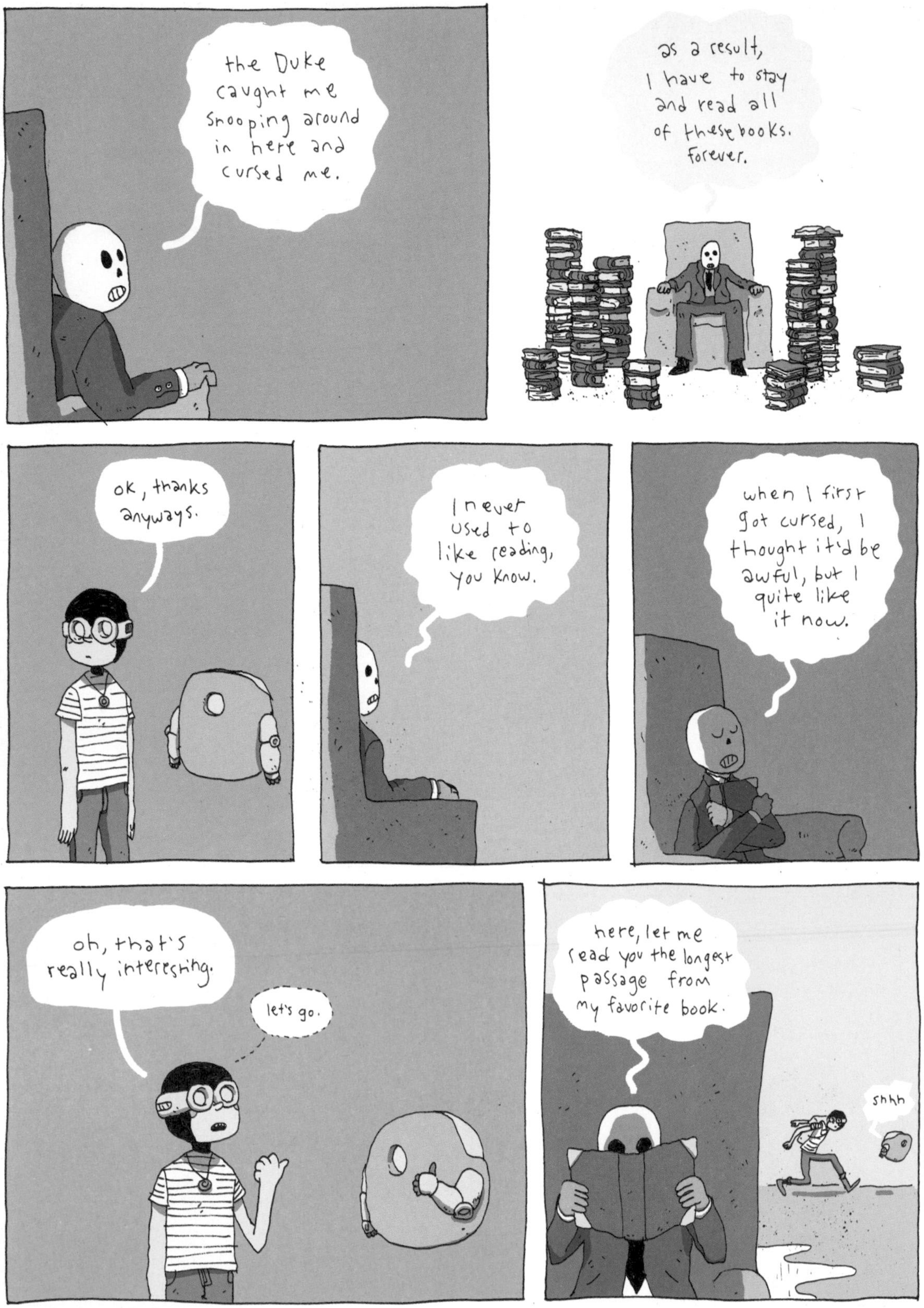
the Duke caught me snooping around in here and cursed me.
as a result, I have to stay and read all of these books. forever.
ok, thanks anyways.
I never used to like reading, you know.
when I first got cursed, I thought it'd be awful, but I quite like it now.
oh, that's really interesting.
let's go.
here, let me read you the longest passage from my favorite book.
shhh

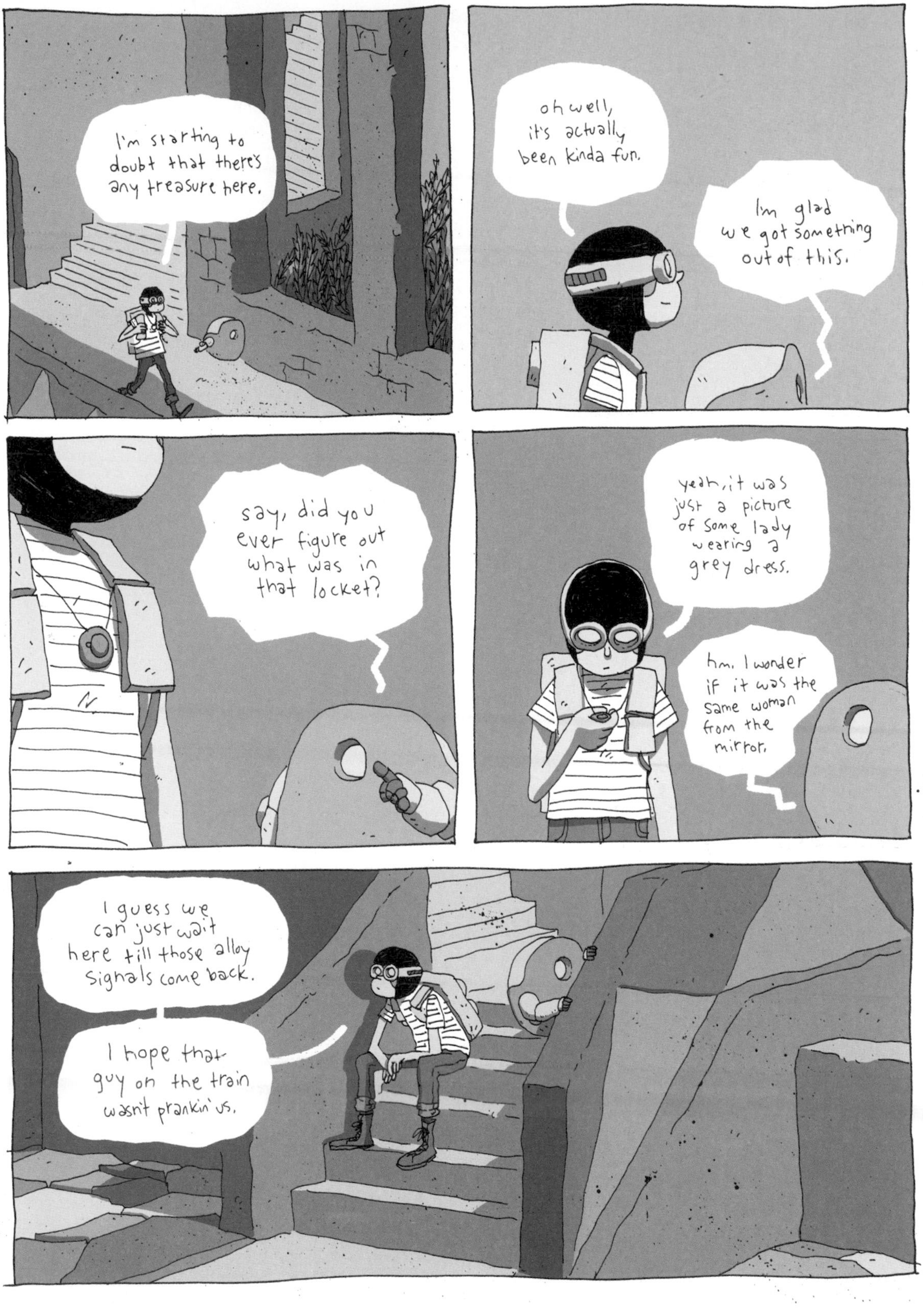
I'm starting to doubt that there's any treasure here.
oh well, it's actually been kinda fun.
I'm glad we got something out of this.
say, did you ever figure out what was in that locket?
yeah, it was just a picture of some lady wearing a grey dress.
hm. I wonder if it was the same woman from the mirror.
I guess we can just wait here till those alloy signals come back.
I hope that guy on the train wasn't prankin' us.

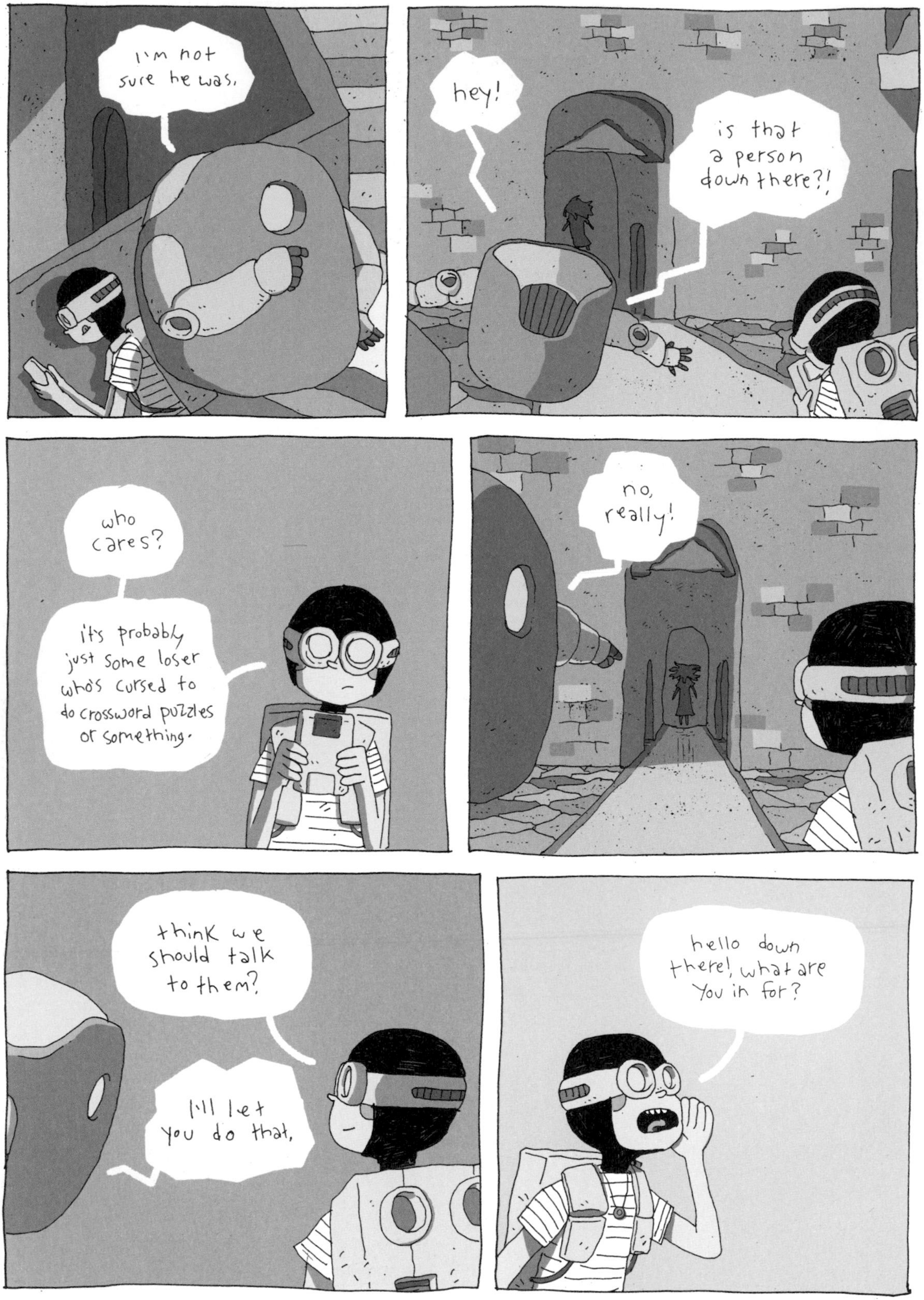
i'm not sure he was.
hey!
is that a person down there?!
who cares?
it's probably just some loser who's cursed to do crossword puzzles or something.
no, really!
think we should talk to them?
i'll let you do that.
hello down there! what are you in for?

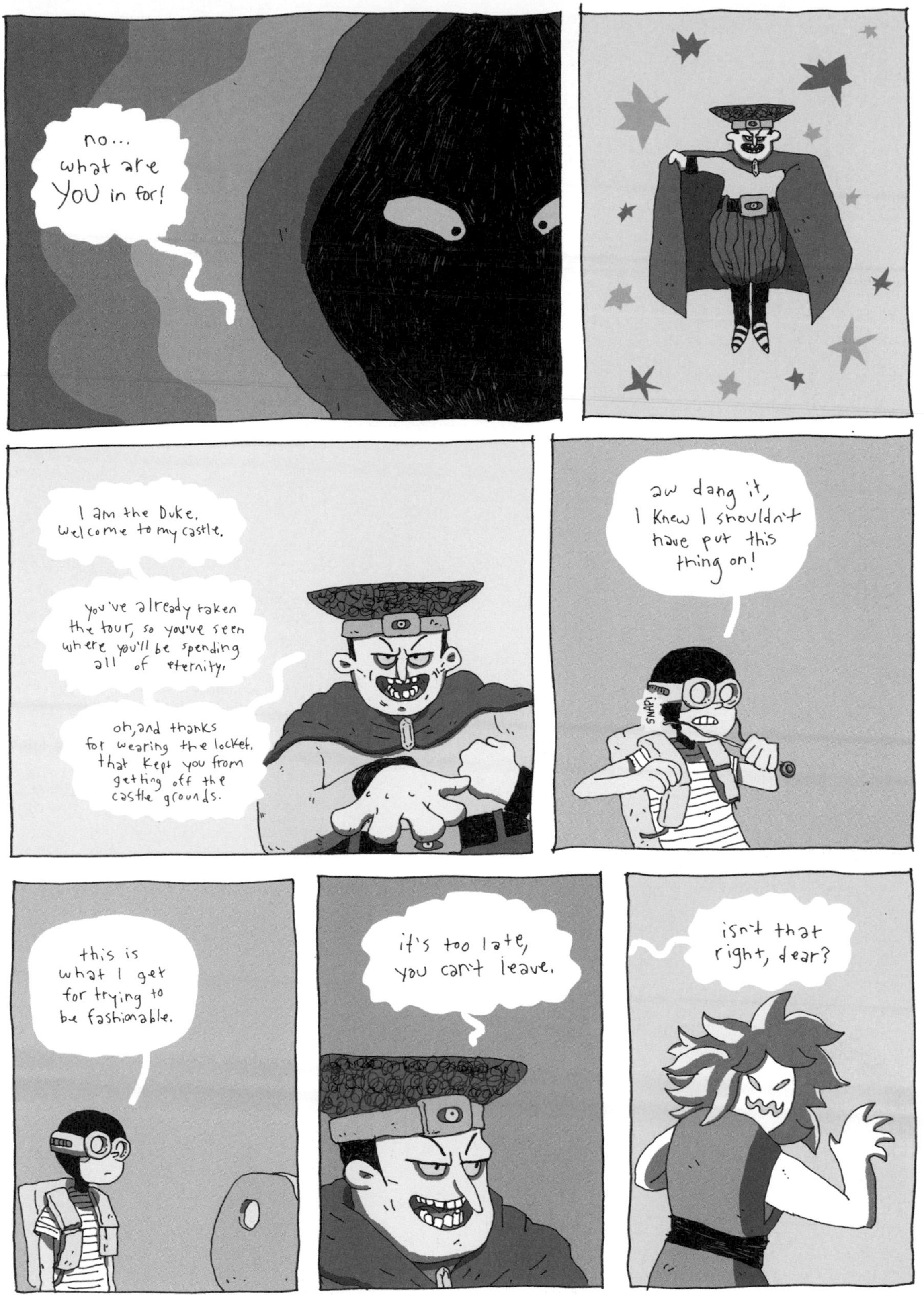
no... what are YOU in for!
I am the Duke. Welcome to my castle.
you've already taken the tour, so you've seen where you'll be spending all of eternity.
oh, and thanks for wearing the locket. that kept you from getting off the castle grounds.
aw dang it, I knew I shouldn't have put this thing on!
SNAP!
this is what I get for trying to be fashionable.
it's too late, you can't leave.
isn't that right, dear?

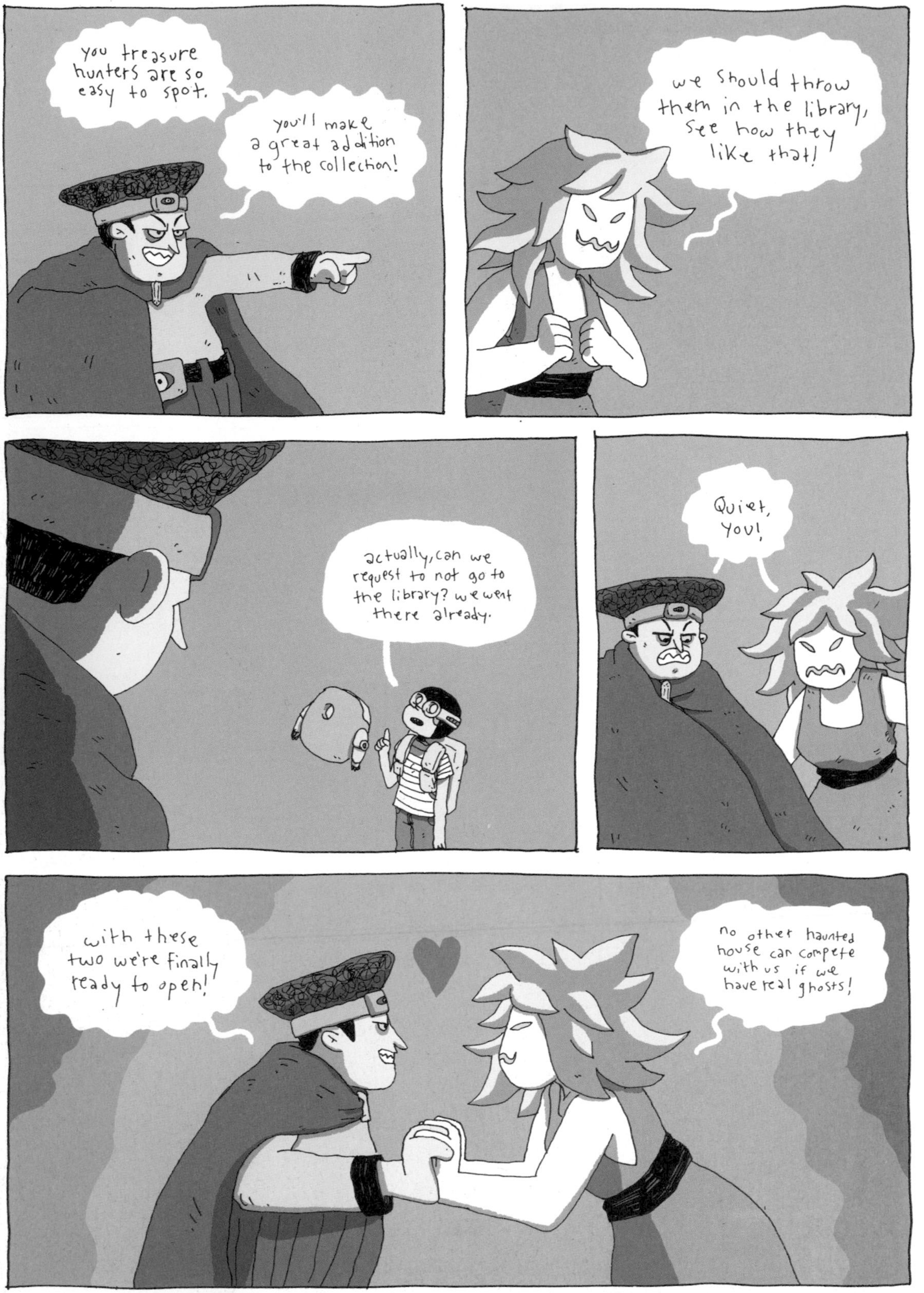
you treasure hunters are so easy to spot.
you'll make a great addition to the collection!
we should throw them in the library, see how they like that!
actually, can we request to not go to the library? we went there already.
Quiet, you!
with these two we're finally ready to open!
no other haunted house can compete with us if we have real ghosts!

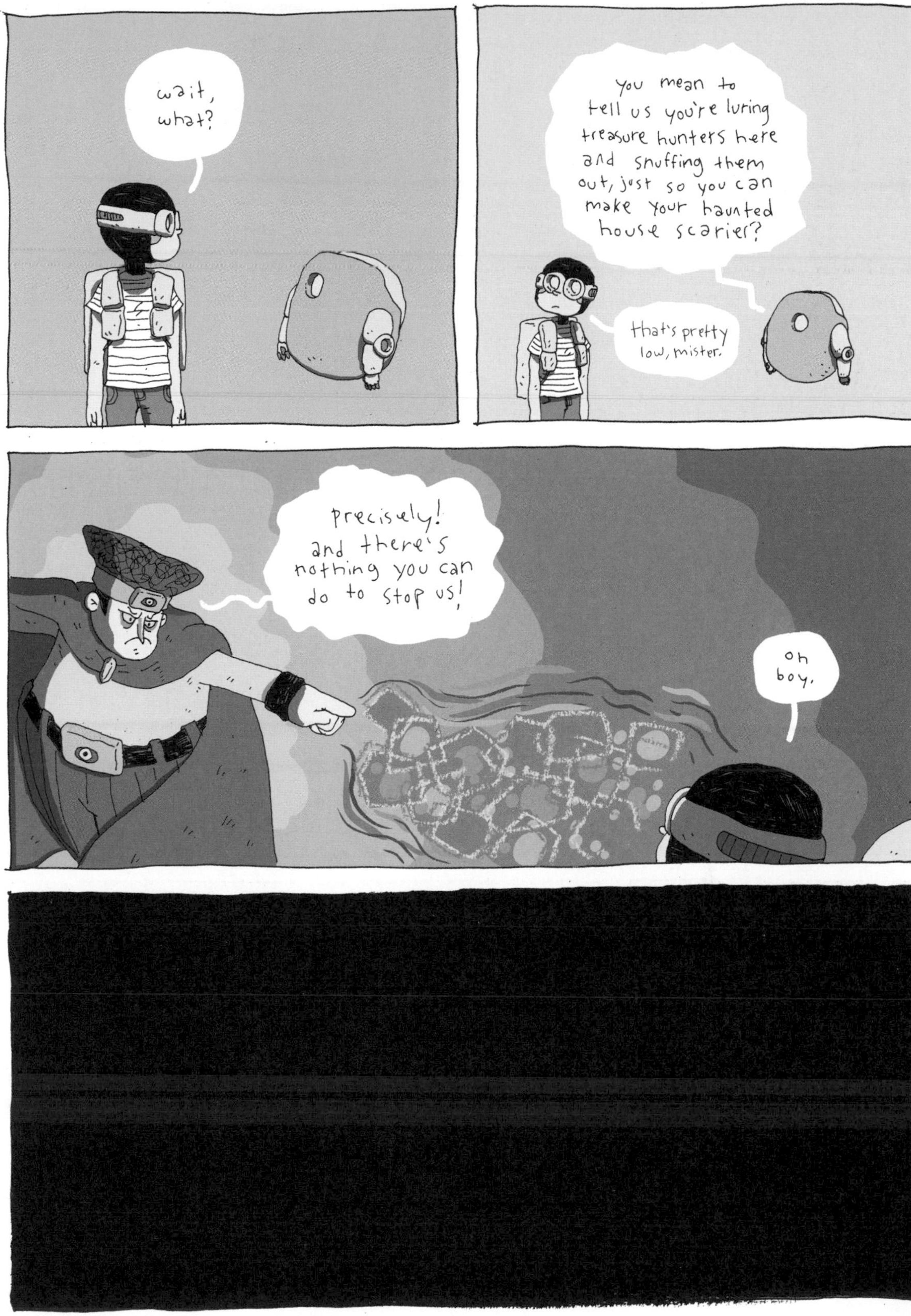
wait, what?
you mean to tell us you're luring treasure hunters here and snuffing them out, just so you can make your haunted house scarier?
that's pretty low, mister.
precisely! and there's nothing you can do to stop us!
oh boy.

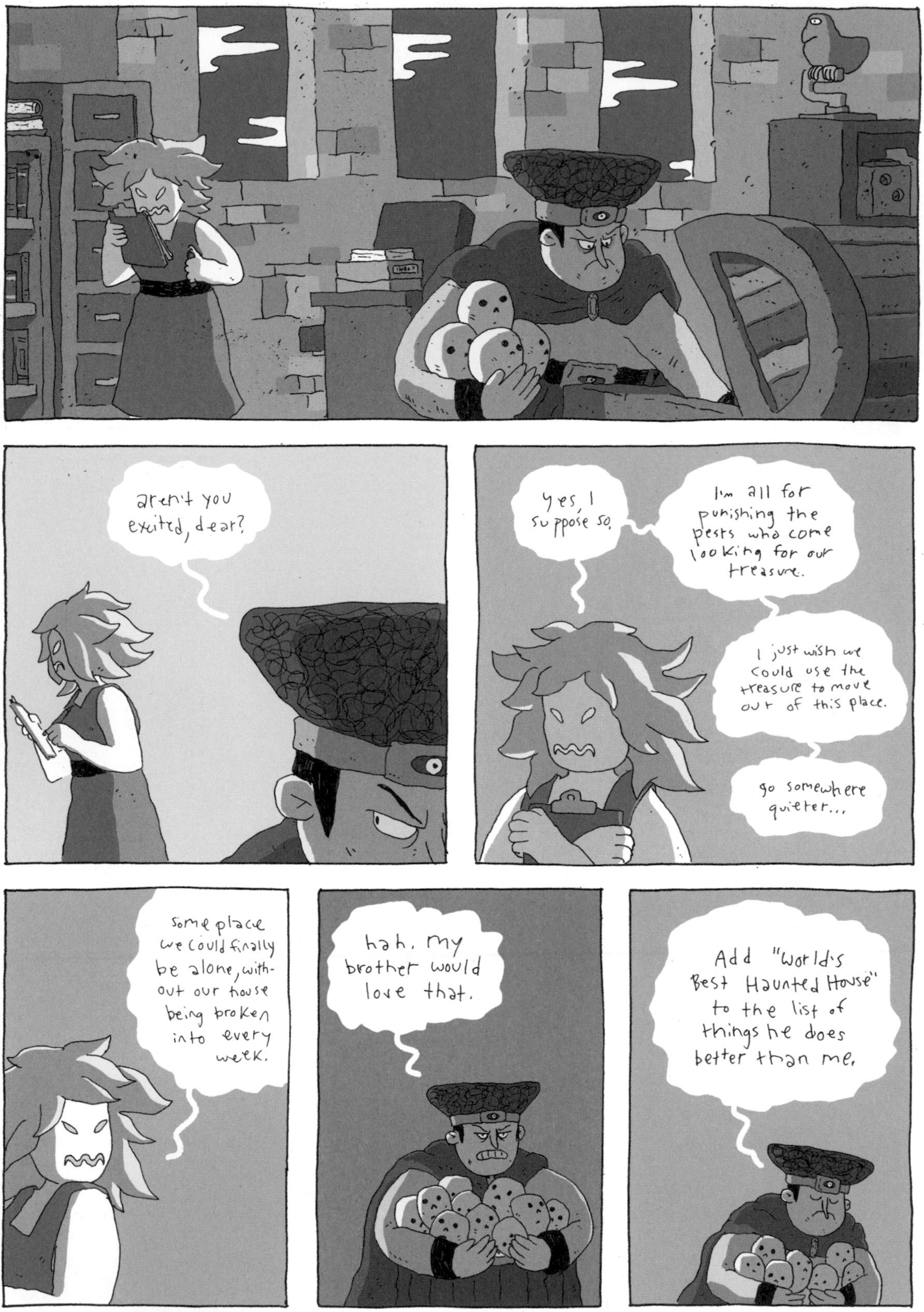
aren't you excited, dear?
yes, I suppose so.
I'm all for punishing the pests who come looking for our treasure.
I just wish we could use the treasure to move out of this place.
go somewhere quieter...
some place we could finally be alone, without our house being broken into every week.
hah. my brother would love that.
Add "World's Best Haunted House" to the list of things he does better than me.

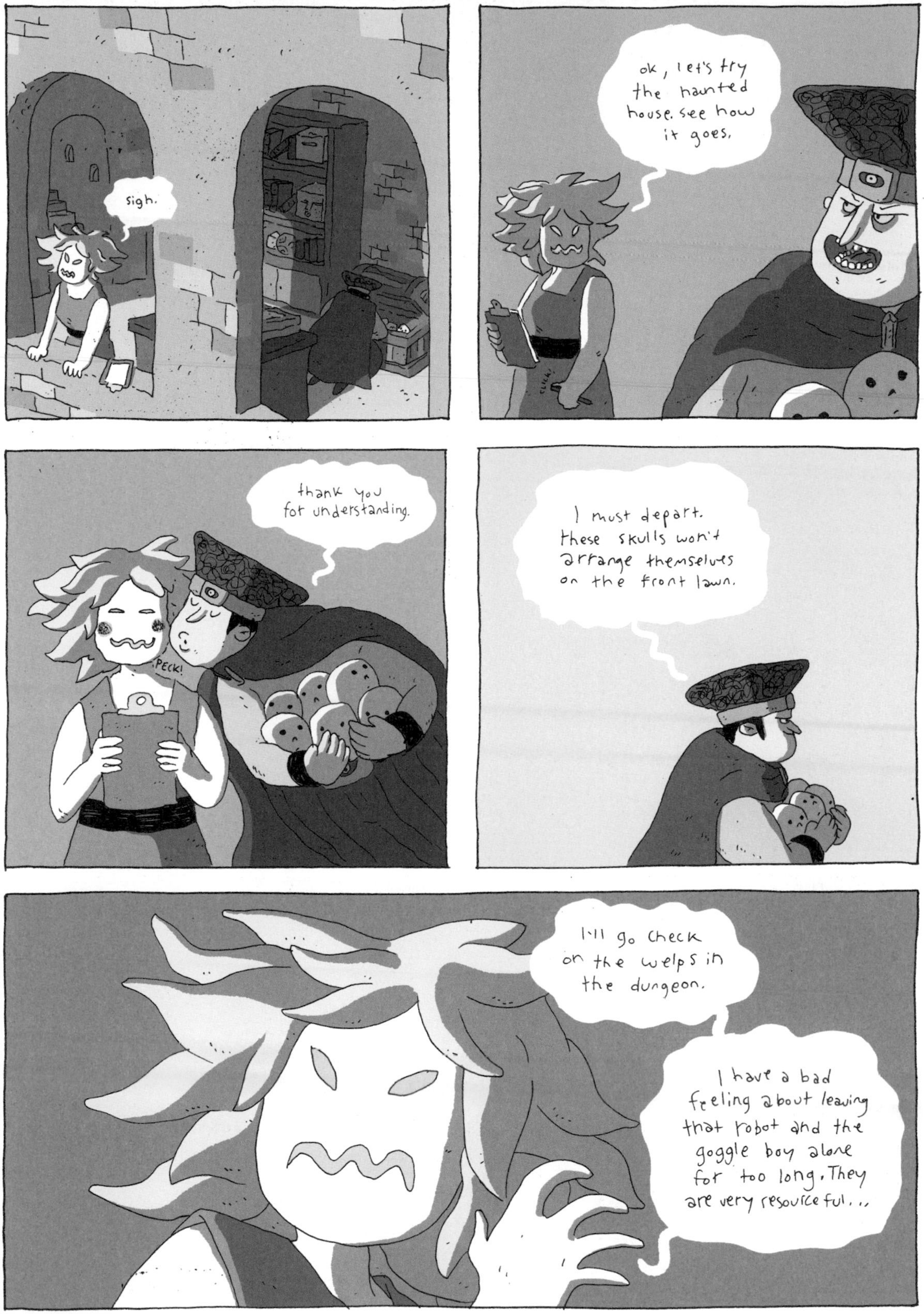
sigh.
ok, let's try the haunted house. see how it goes.
thank you for understanding.
PECK!
I must depart. these skulls won't arrange themselves on the front lawn.
I'll go check on the welps in the dungeon.
I have a bad feeling about leaving that robot and the goggle boy alone for too long. They are very resourceful...

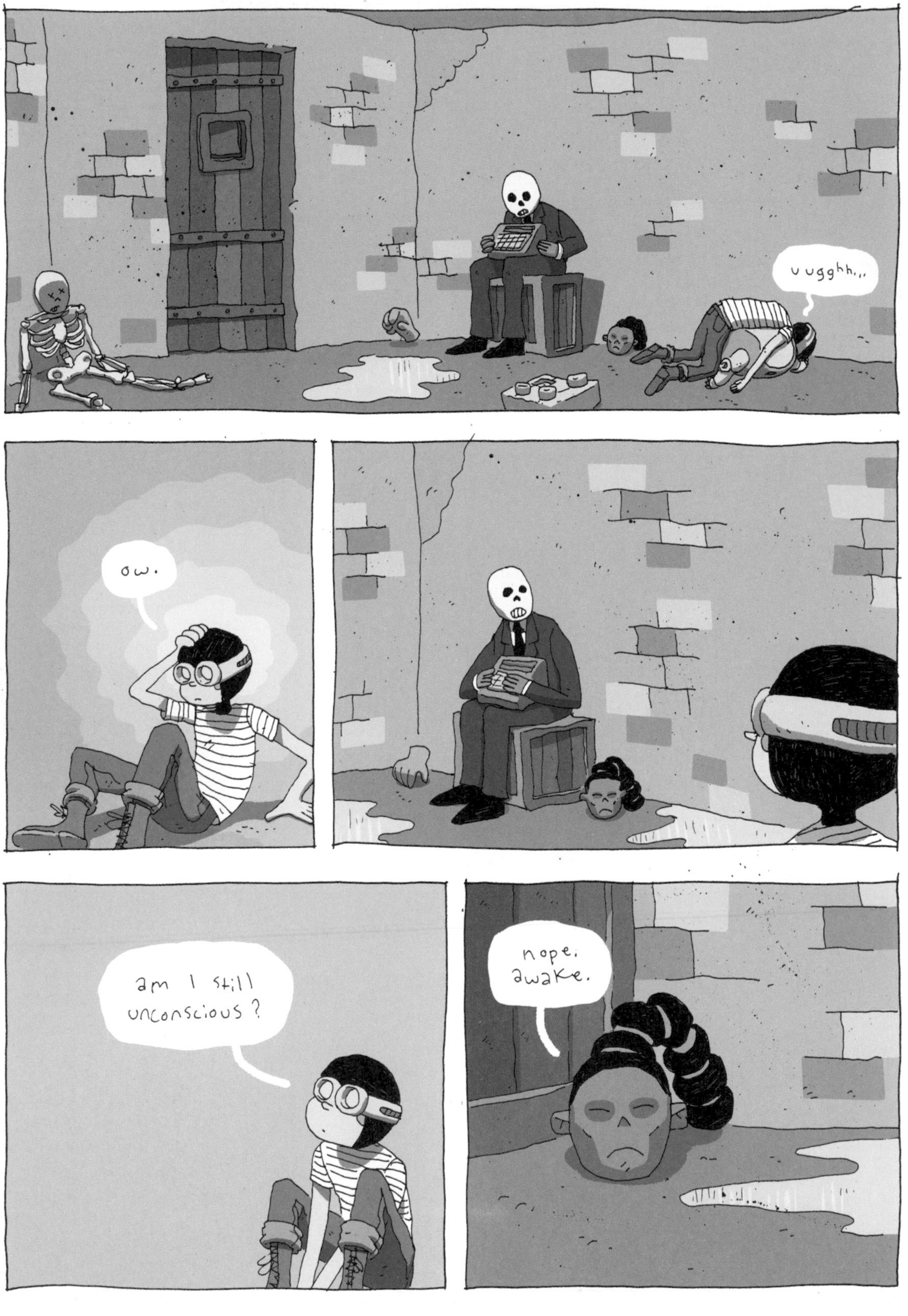
uugghh...
ow.
am I still unconscious?
nope. awake.

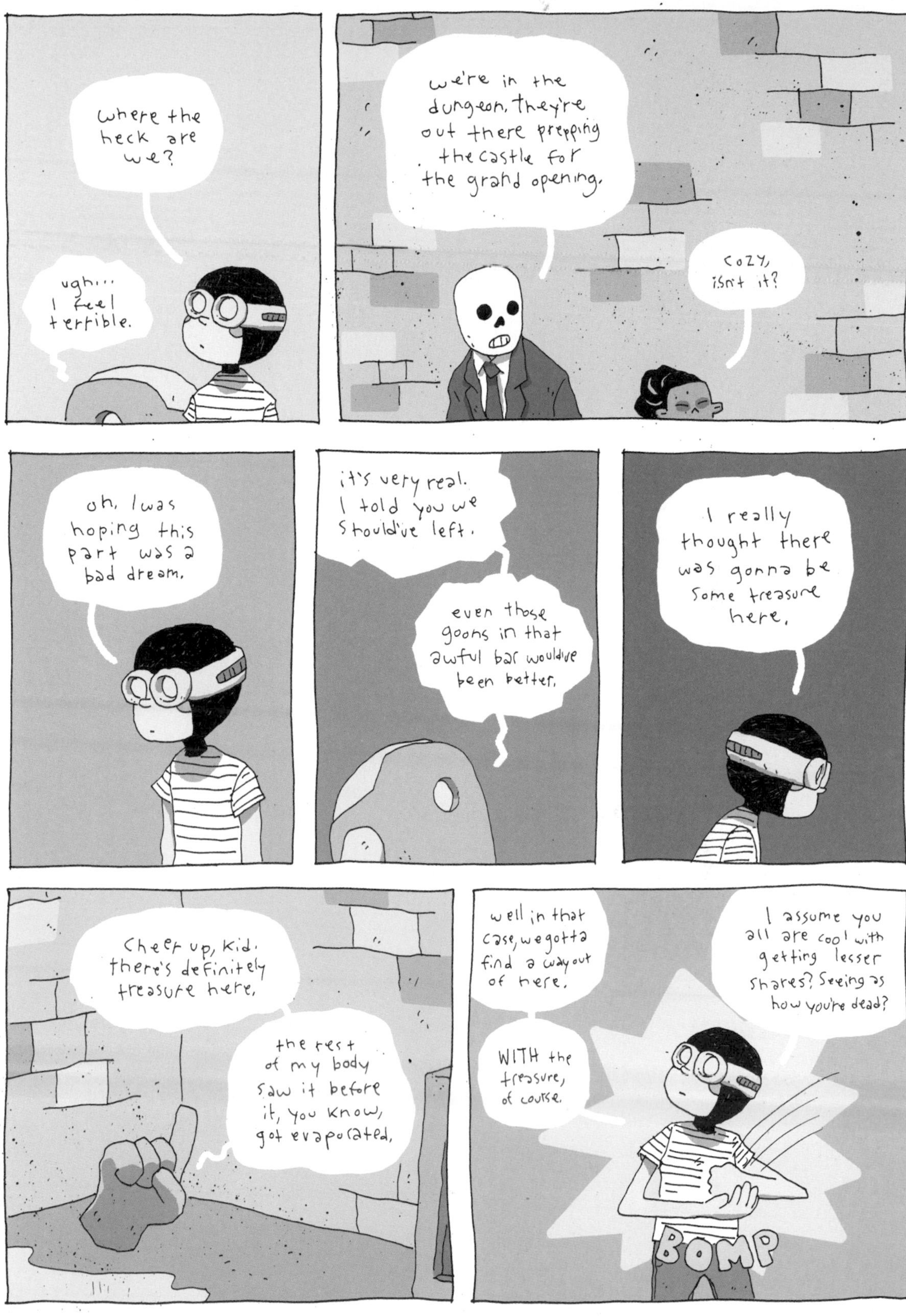
where the heck are we?
ugh... I feel terrible.
we're in the dungeon, they're out there prepping the castle for the grand opening.
cozy, isn't it?
oh, I was hoping this part was a bad dream.
it's very real. I told you we should've left.
even those goons in that awful bar would've been better.
I really thought there was gonna be some treasure here.
Cheer up, kid. there's definitely treasure here.
the rest of my body saw it before it, you know, got evaporated.
well in that case, we gotta find a way out of here.
WITH the treasure, of course.
I assume you all are cool with getting lesser shares? Seeing as how you're dead?
BOMP

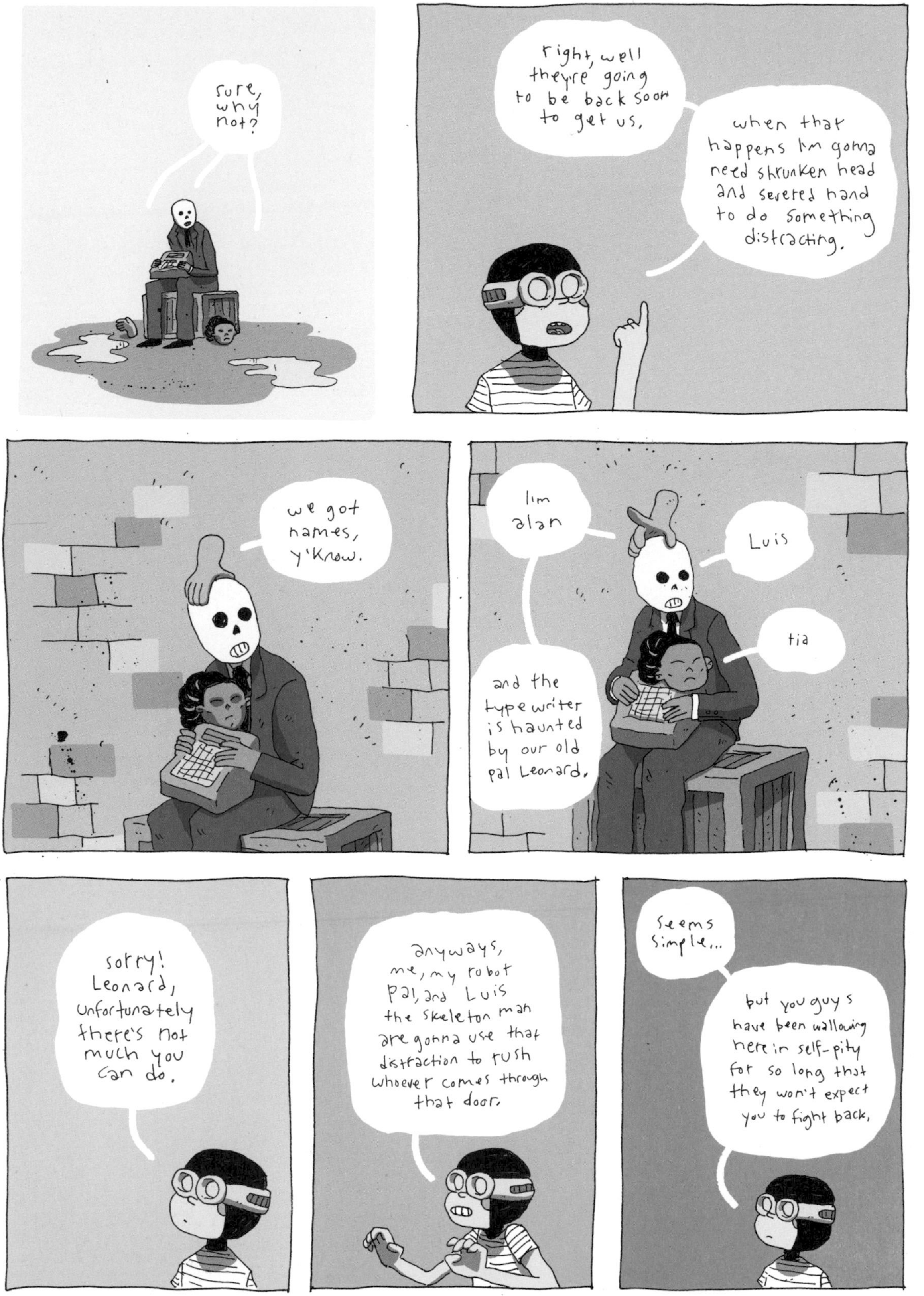
sure, why not?
right, well they're going to be back soon to get us.
when that happens I'm gonna need shrunken head and severed hand to do something distracting.
we got names, y'know.
I'm alan
Luis
tia
and the typewriter is haunted by our old pal Leonard.
sorry! Leonard, unfortunately there's not much you can do.
anyways, me, my robot pal, and Luis the skeleton man are gonna use that distraction to rush whoever comes through that door.
seems simple...
but you guys have been wallowing here in self-pity for so long that they won't expect you to fight back.

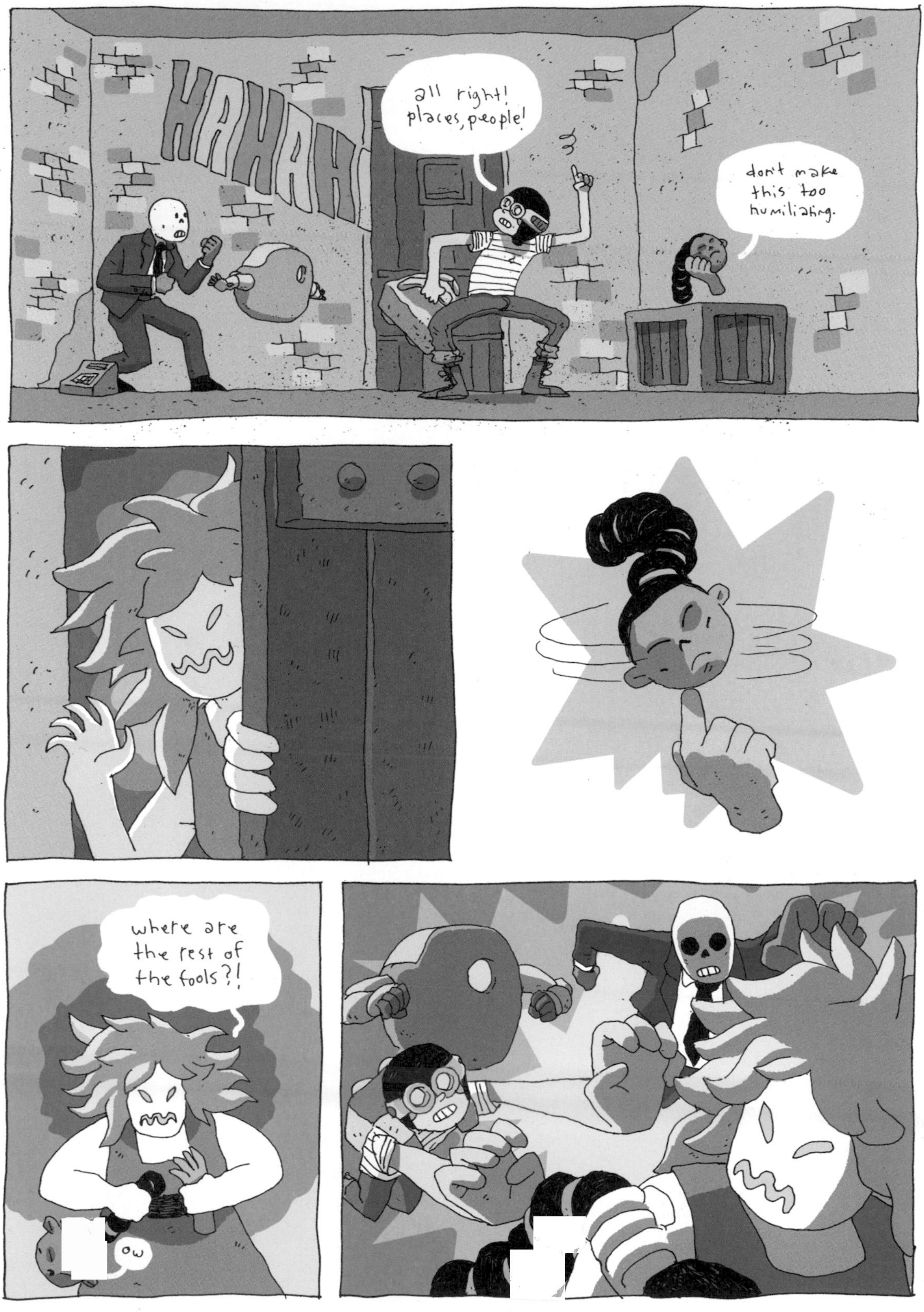
HAHAH!
all right! places, people!
don't make this too humiliating.
where are the rest of the fools?!
ow

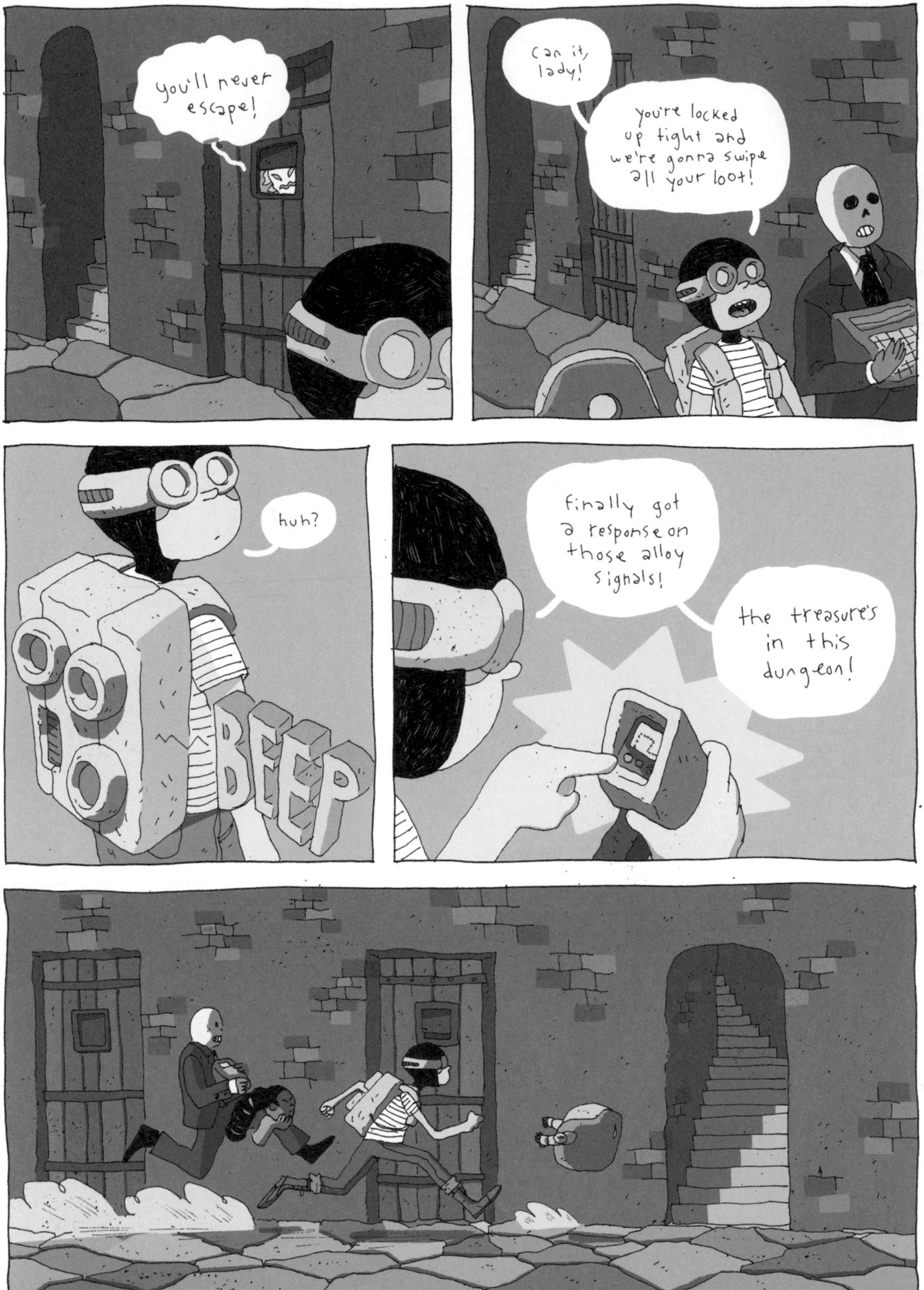

you'll never escape!
can it, lady!
you're locked up tight and we're gonna swipe all your loot!
BEEP
huh?
finally got a response on those alloy signals!
the treasure's in this dungeon!

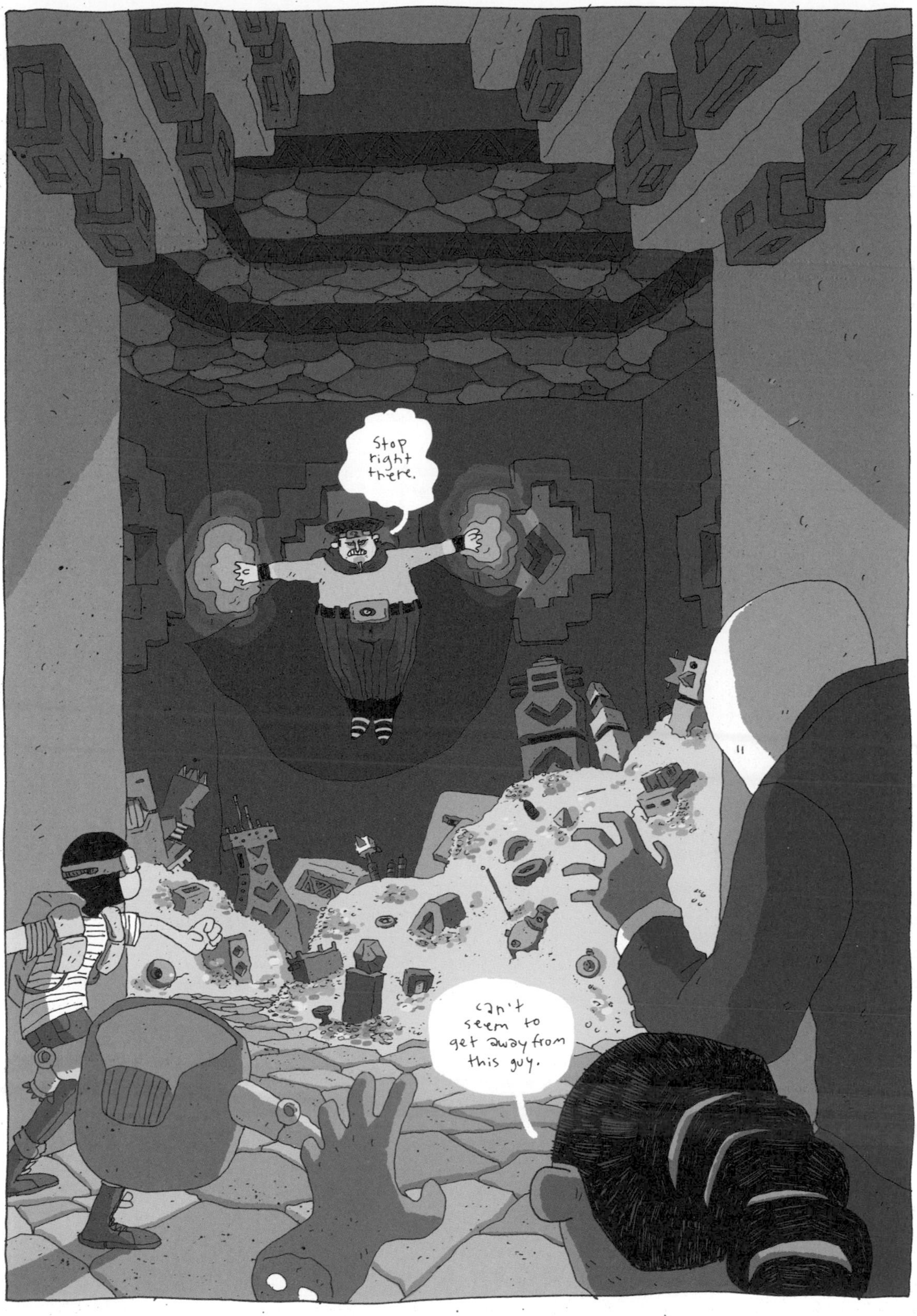
Stop right there.
can't seem to get away from this guy.

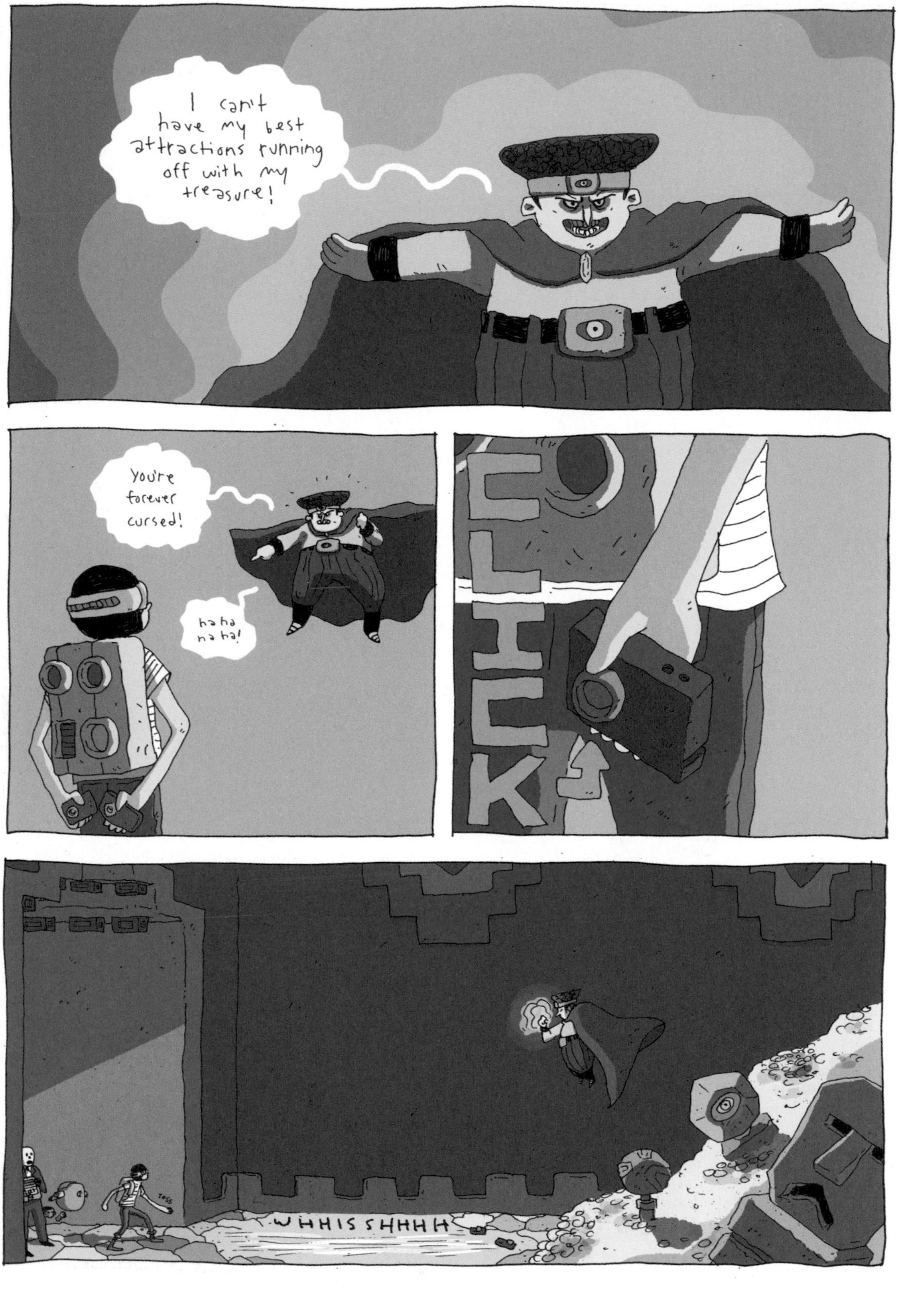
I can't have my best attractions running off with my treasure!
you're forever cursed!
ha ha ha ha!
CLICK
TOSS
WHHISSHHHH

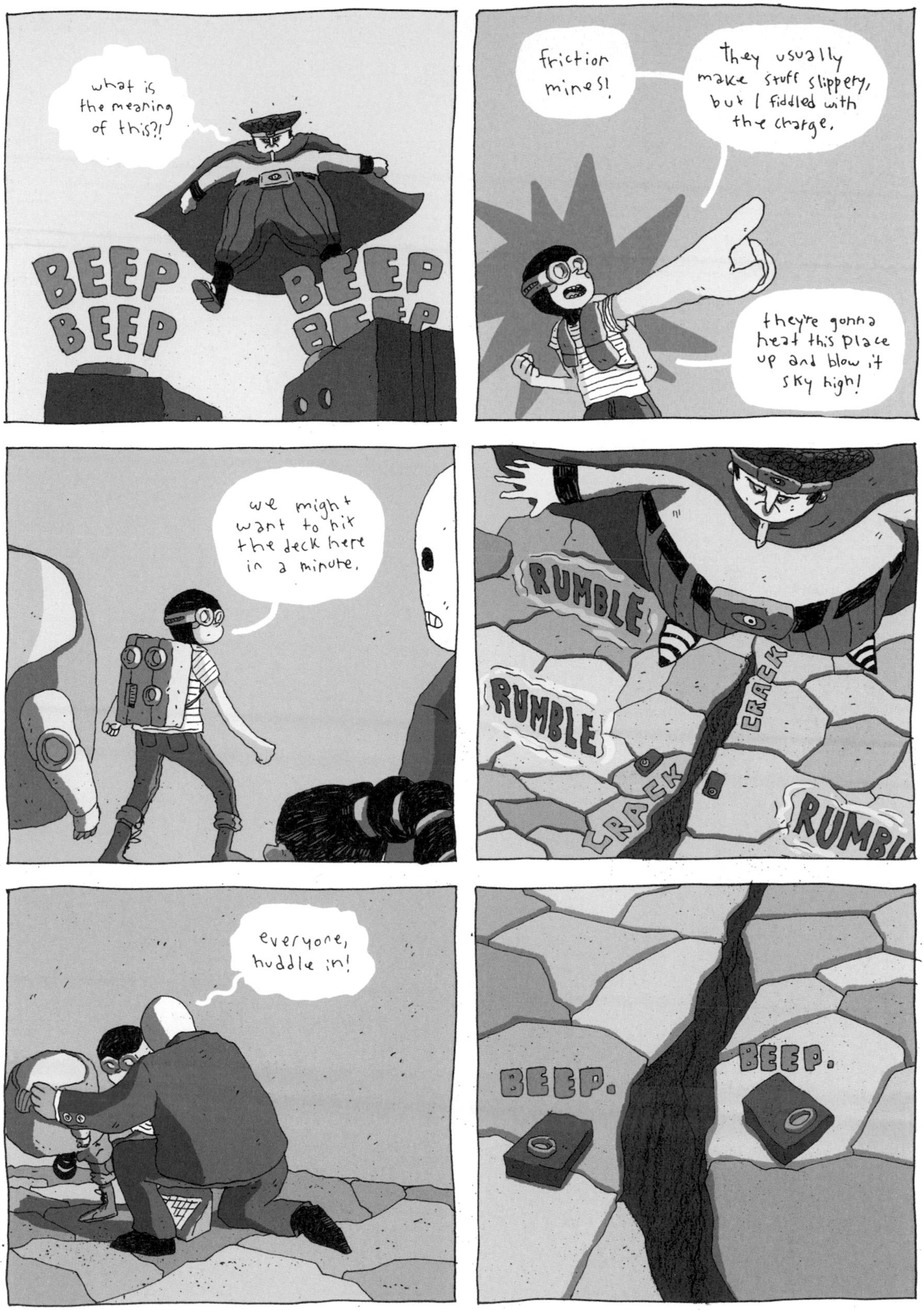
what is the meaning of this?!
BEEP BEEP
BEEP BEEP
friction mines!
They usually make stuff slippery, but I fiddled with the charge.
they're gonna heat this place up and blow it sky high!
we might want to hit the deck here in a minute.
RUMBLE
RUMBLE
CRACK
CRACK
everyone, huddle in!
BEEP.
BEEP.

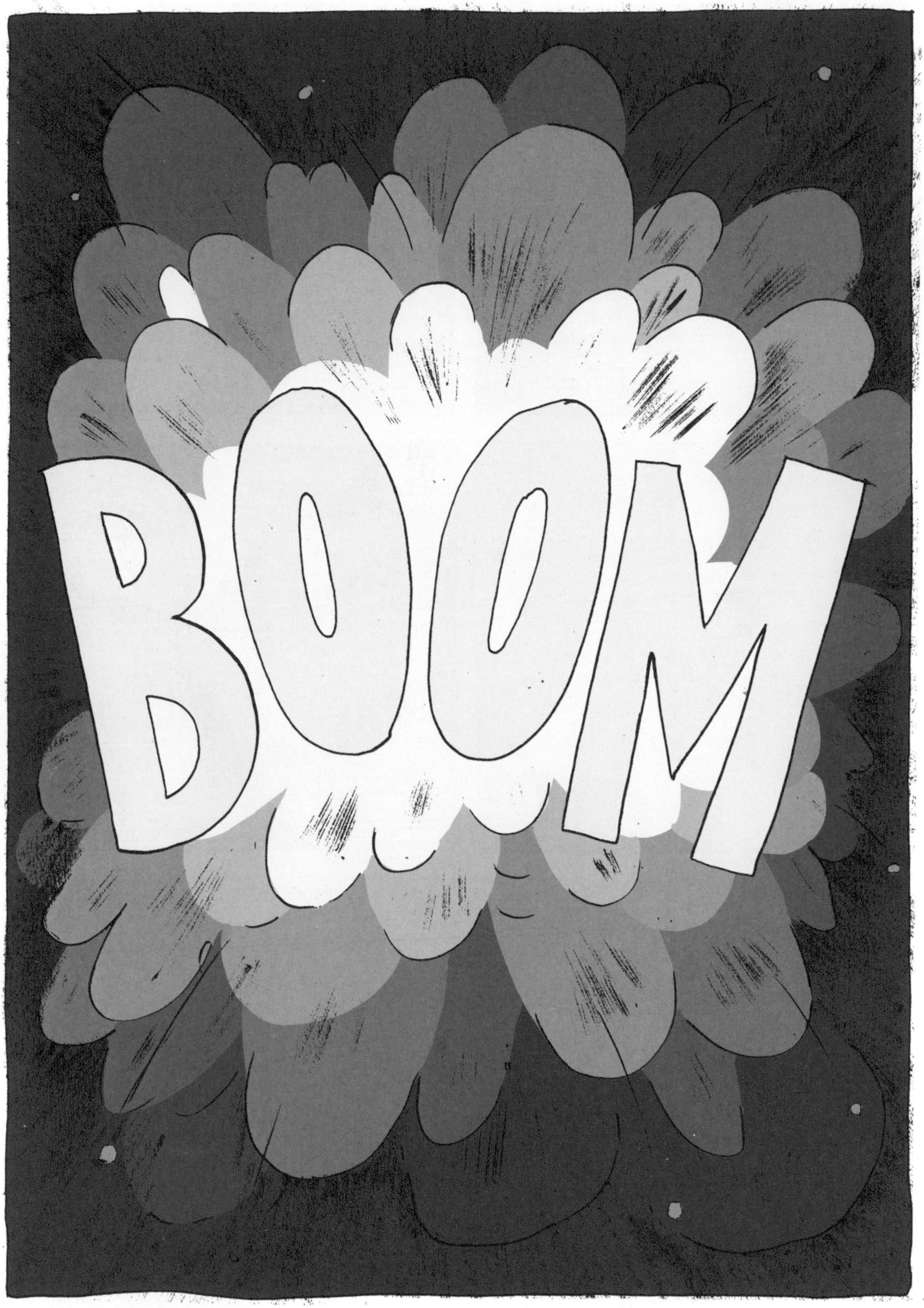
BOOM

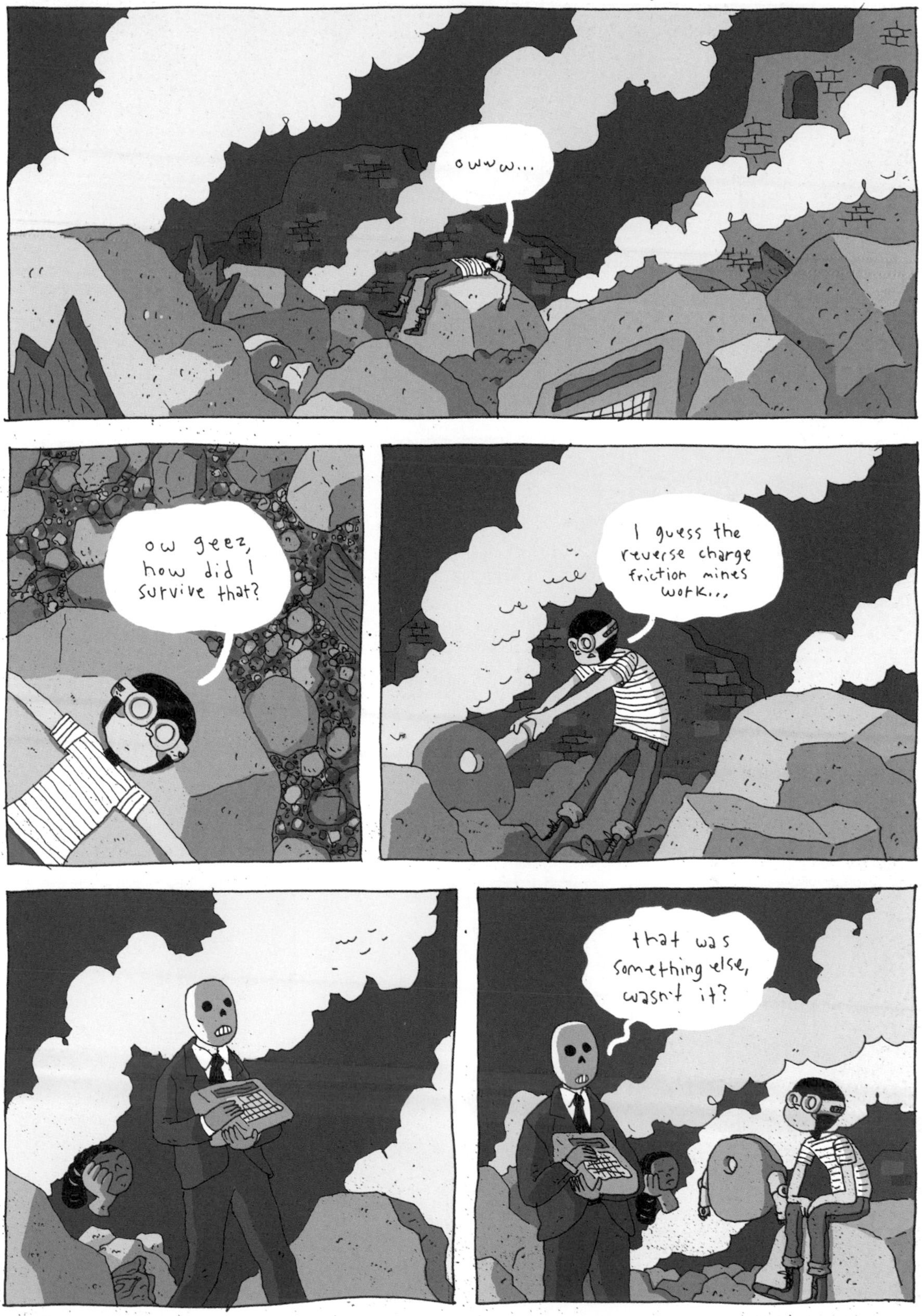
owww...
ow geez, how did I survive that?
I guess the reverse charge friction mines work...
that was something else, wasn't it?

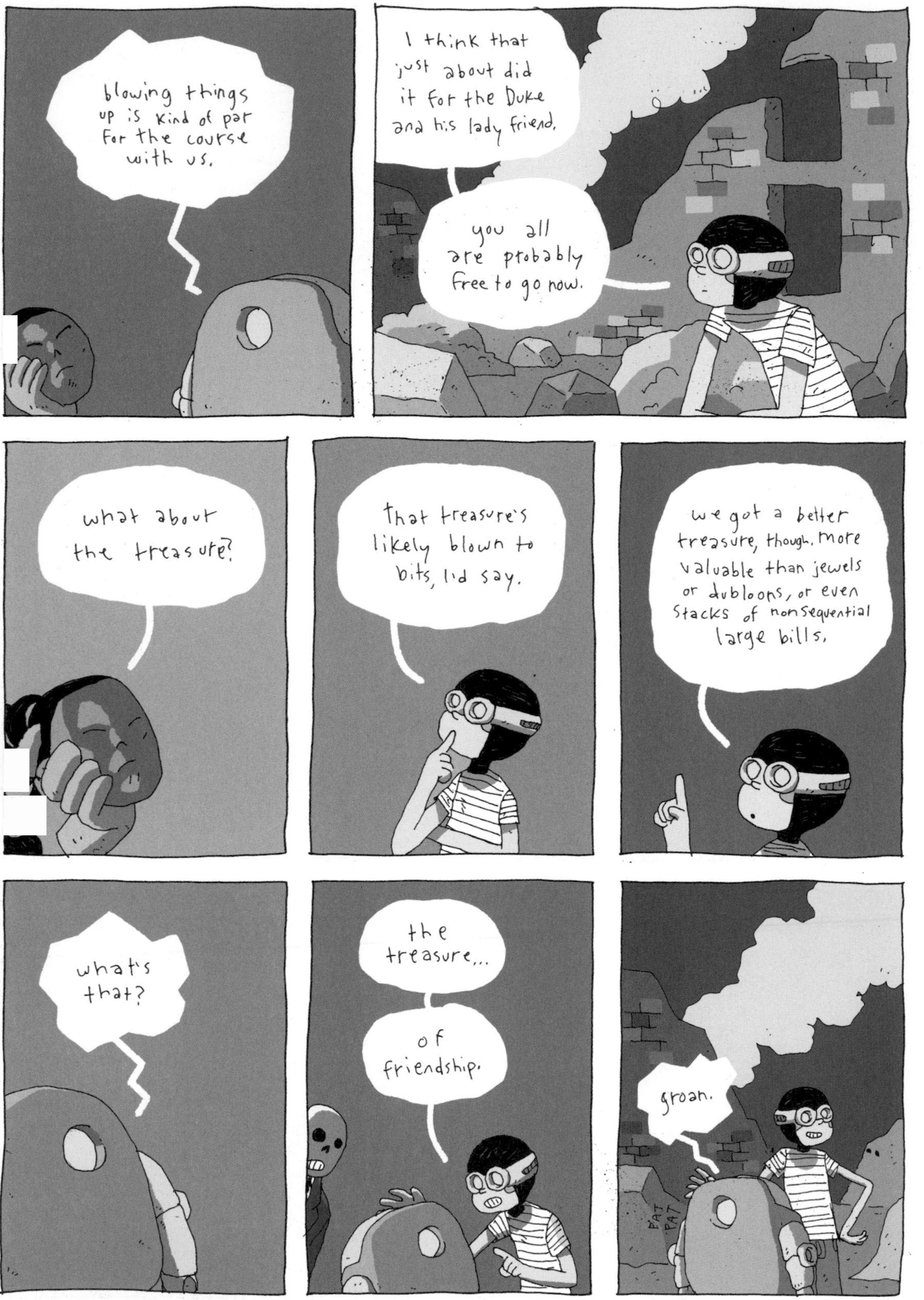

blowing things up is kind of par for the course with us.
I think that just about did it for the Duke and his lady friend.
you all are probably free to go now.
what about the treasure?
that treasure's likely blown to bits, I'd say.
we got a better treasure, though. more valuable than jewels or dubloons, or even stacks of nonsequential large bills.
what's that?
the treasure...
of friendship.
groan.
PAT PAT

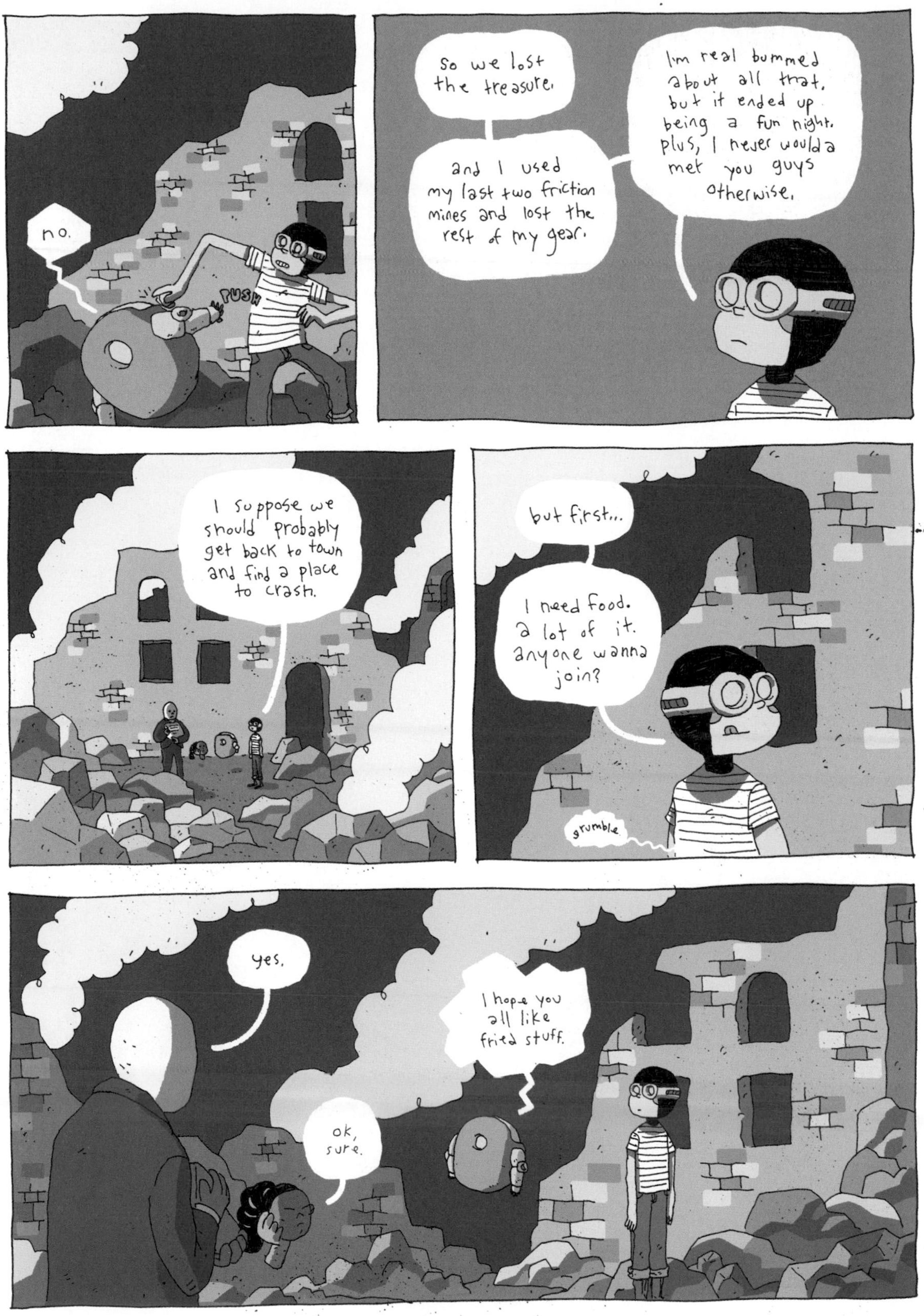
no.
PUSH
so we lost the treasure.
and I used my last two friction mines and lost the rest of my gear.
I'm real bummed about all that, but it ended up being a fun night. plus, I never woulda met you guys otherwise.
I suppose we should probably get back to town and find a place to crash.
but first...
I need food. a lot of it. anyone wanna join?
grumble
yes.
ok, sure.
I hope you all like fried stuff.

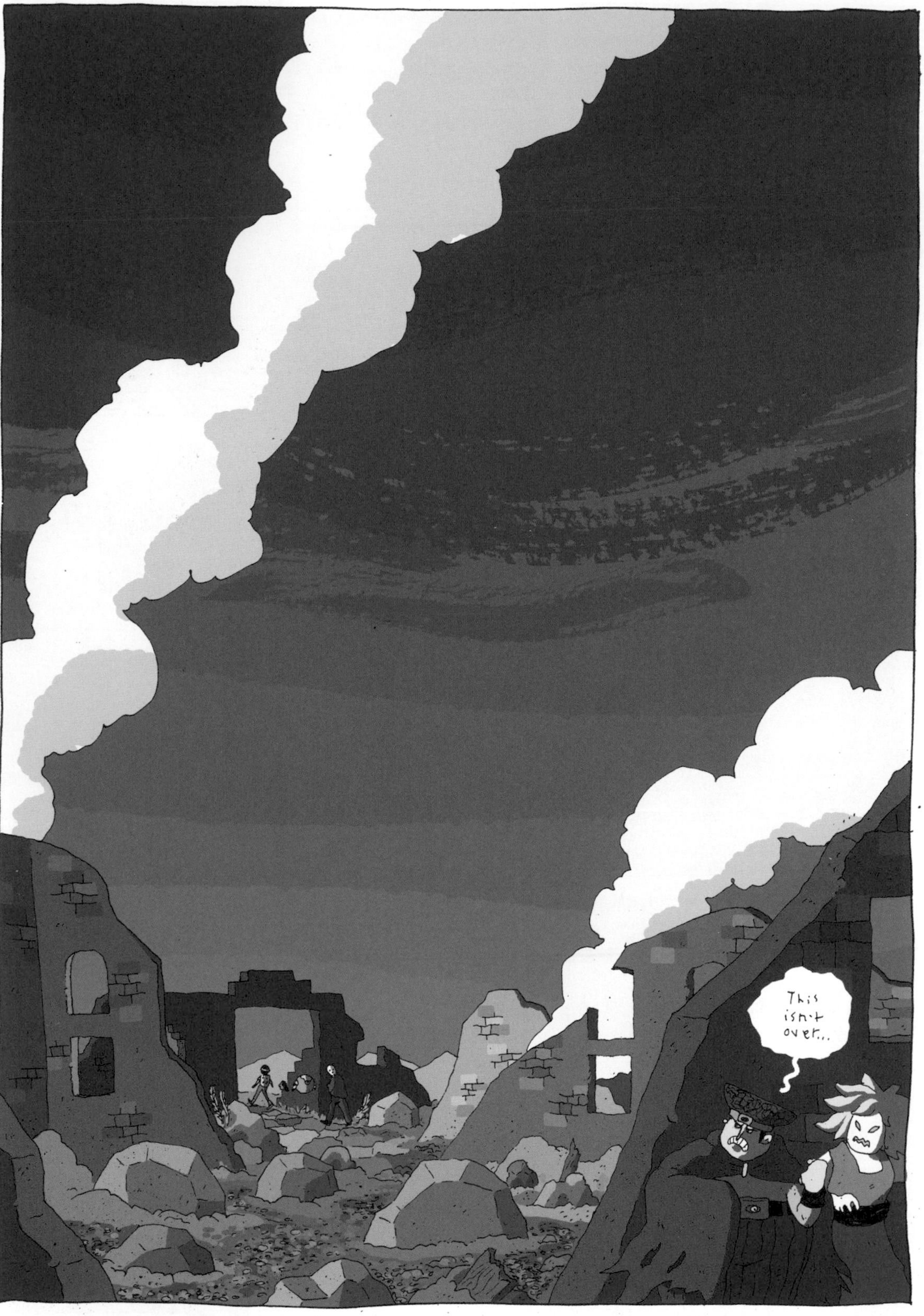
This isn't over...

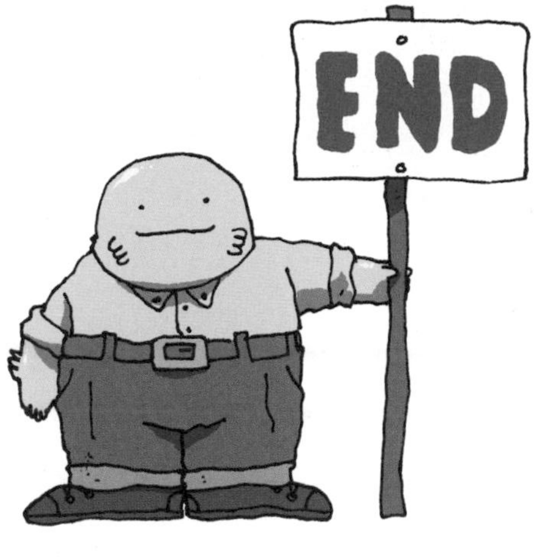
END

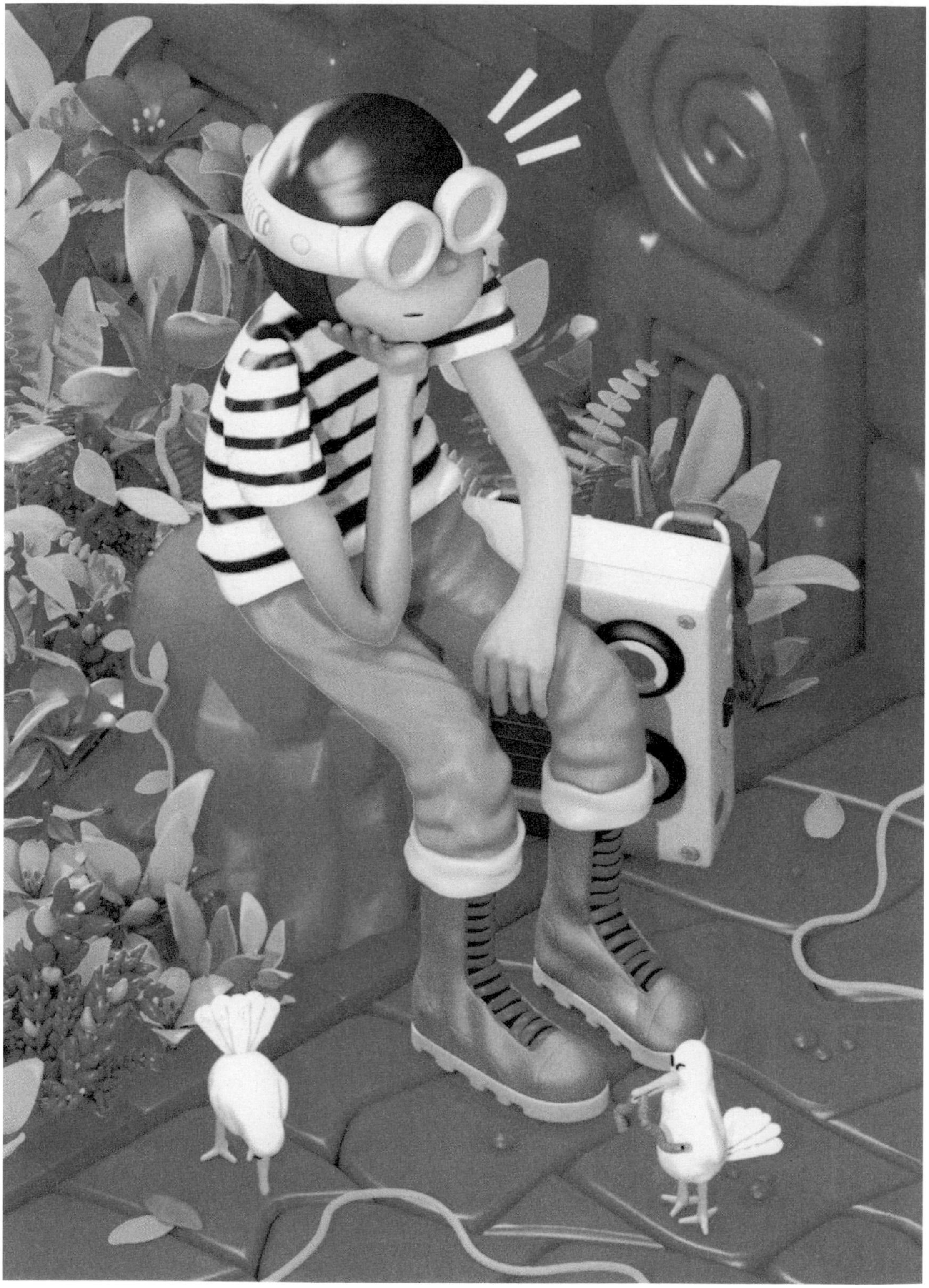

jordan speer

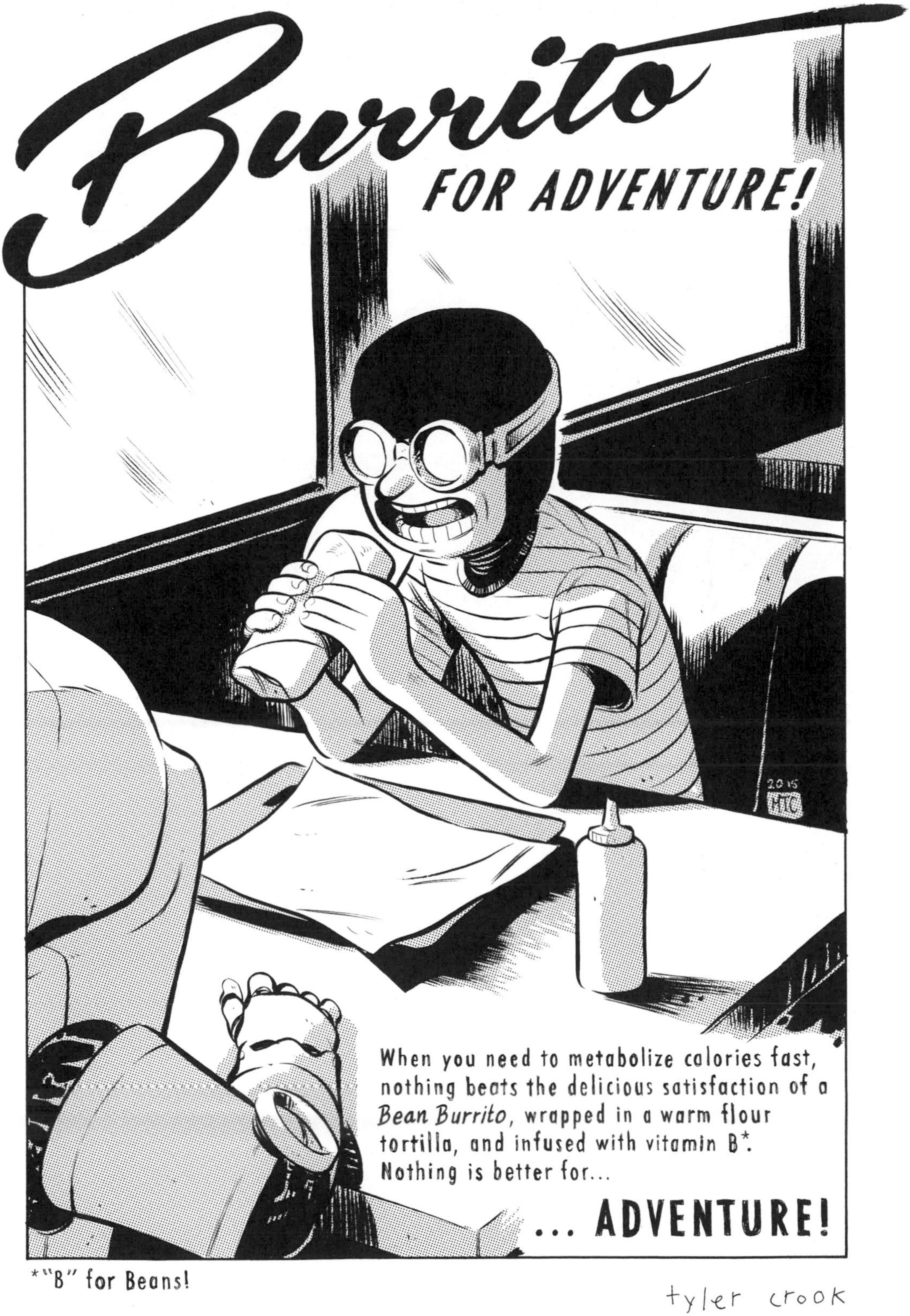
Burrito
FOR ADVENTURE!
2015
HTC
When you need to metabolize calories fast, nothing beats the delicious satisfaction of a *Bean Burrito*, wrapped in a warm flour tortilla, and infused with vitamin B*. Nothing is better for...
... ADVENTURE!

*"B" for Beans!

tyler crook

luis yang + ben sears

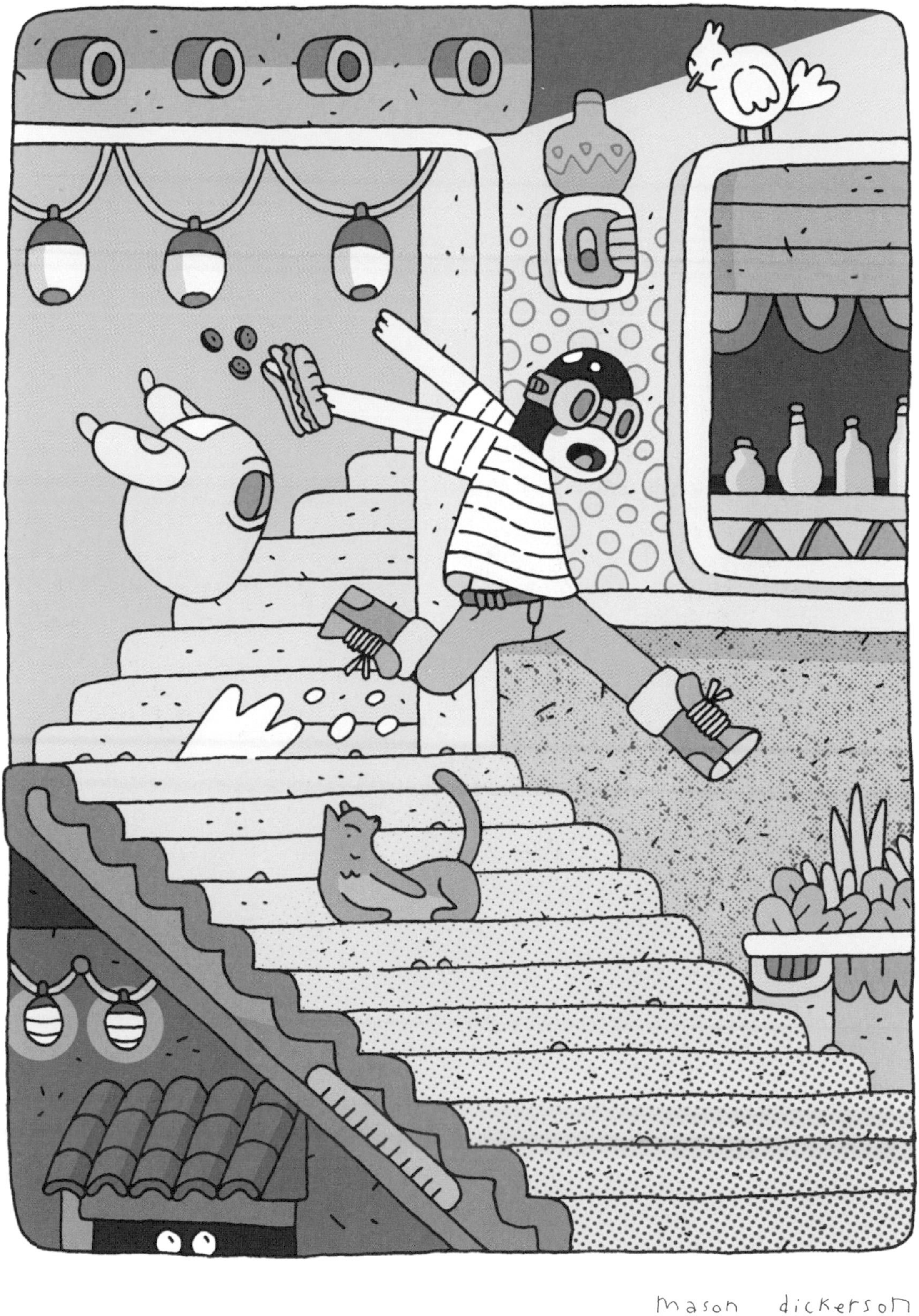

mason dickerson

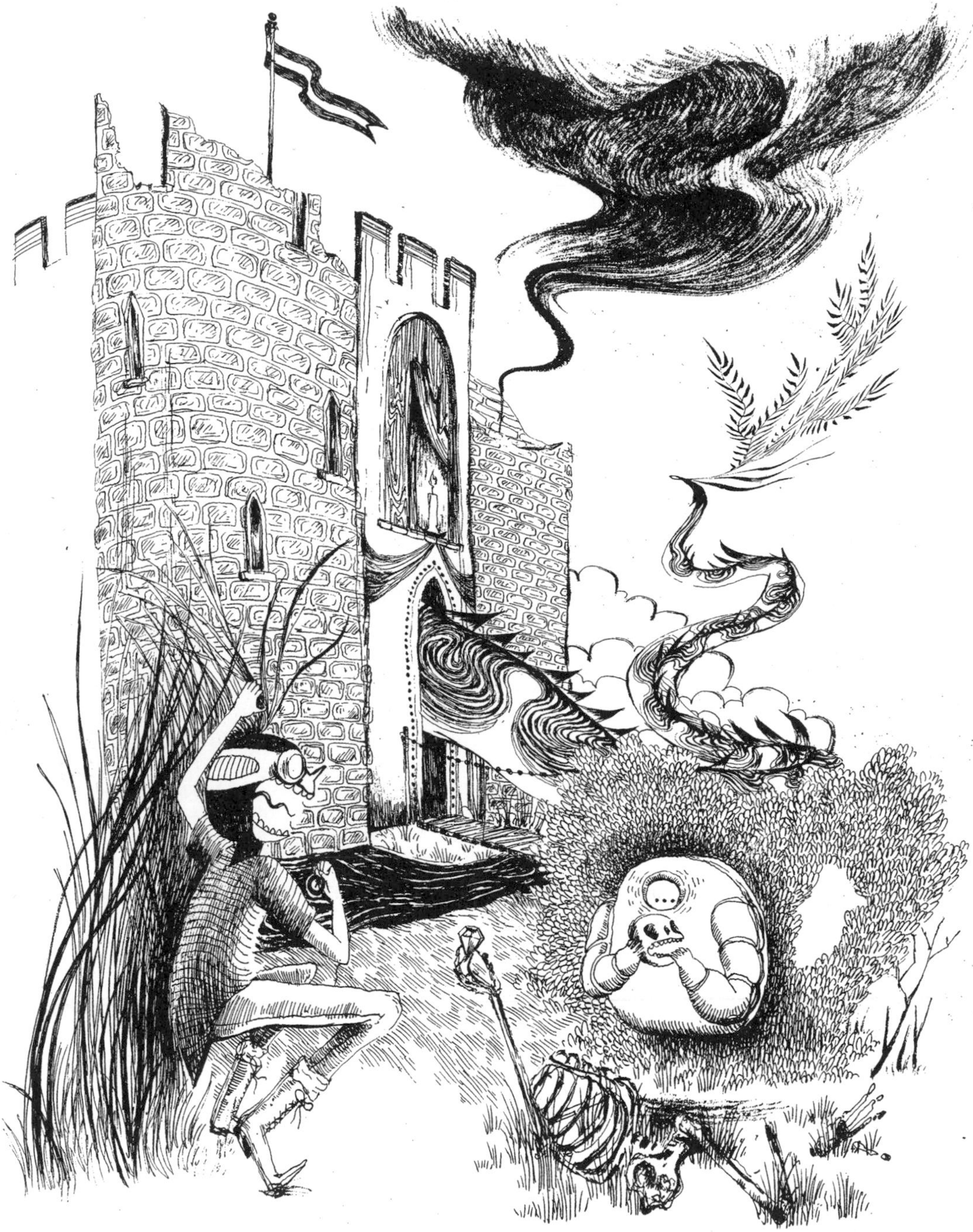

Catherine ho

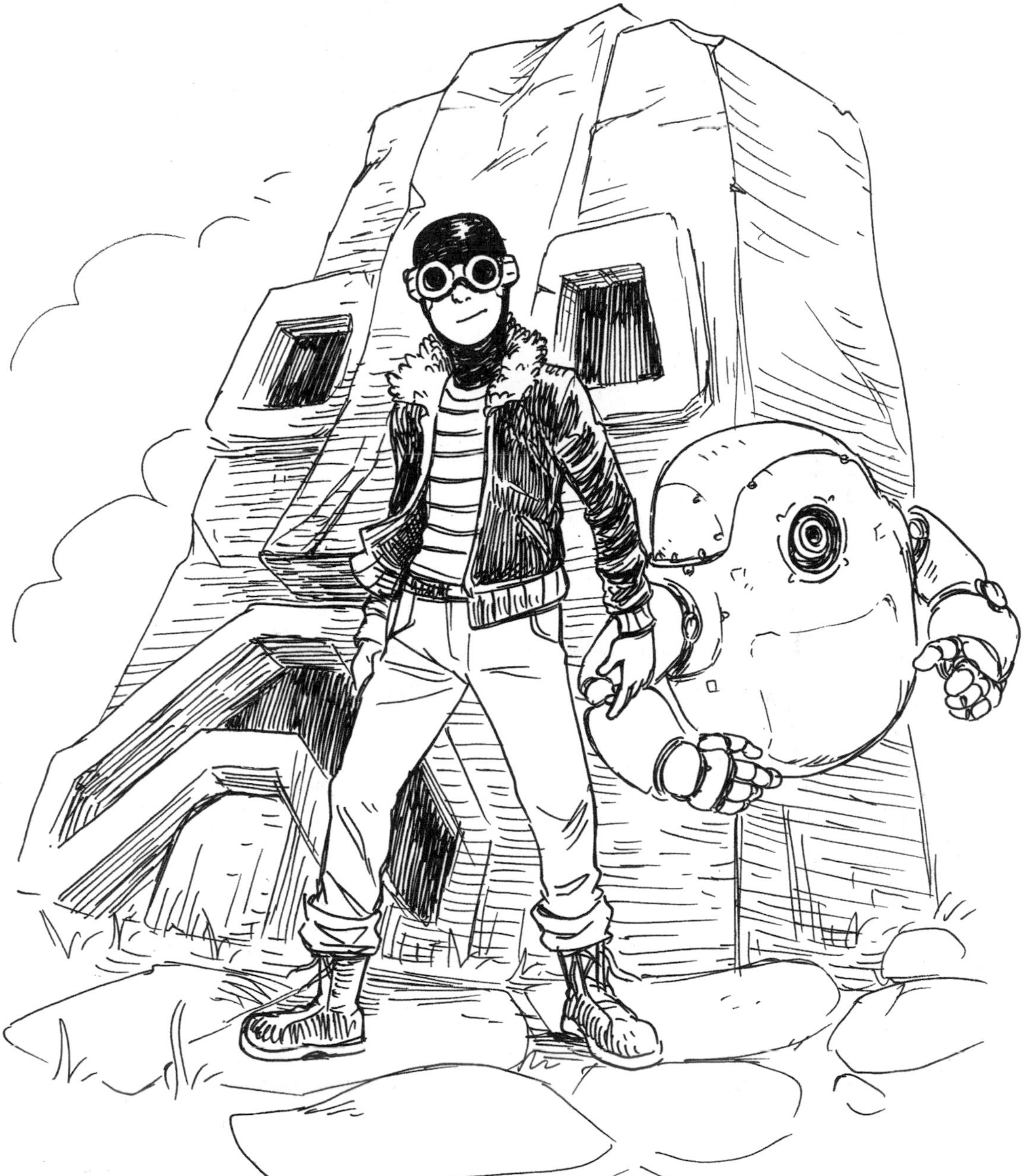

peter wartman

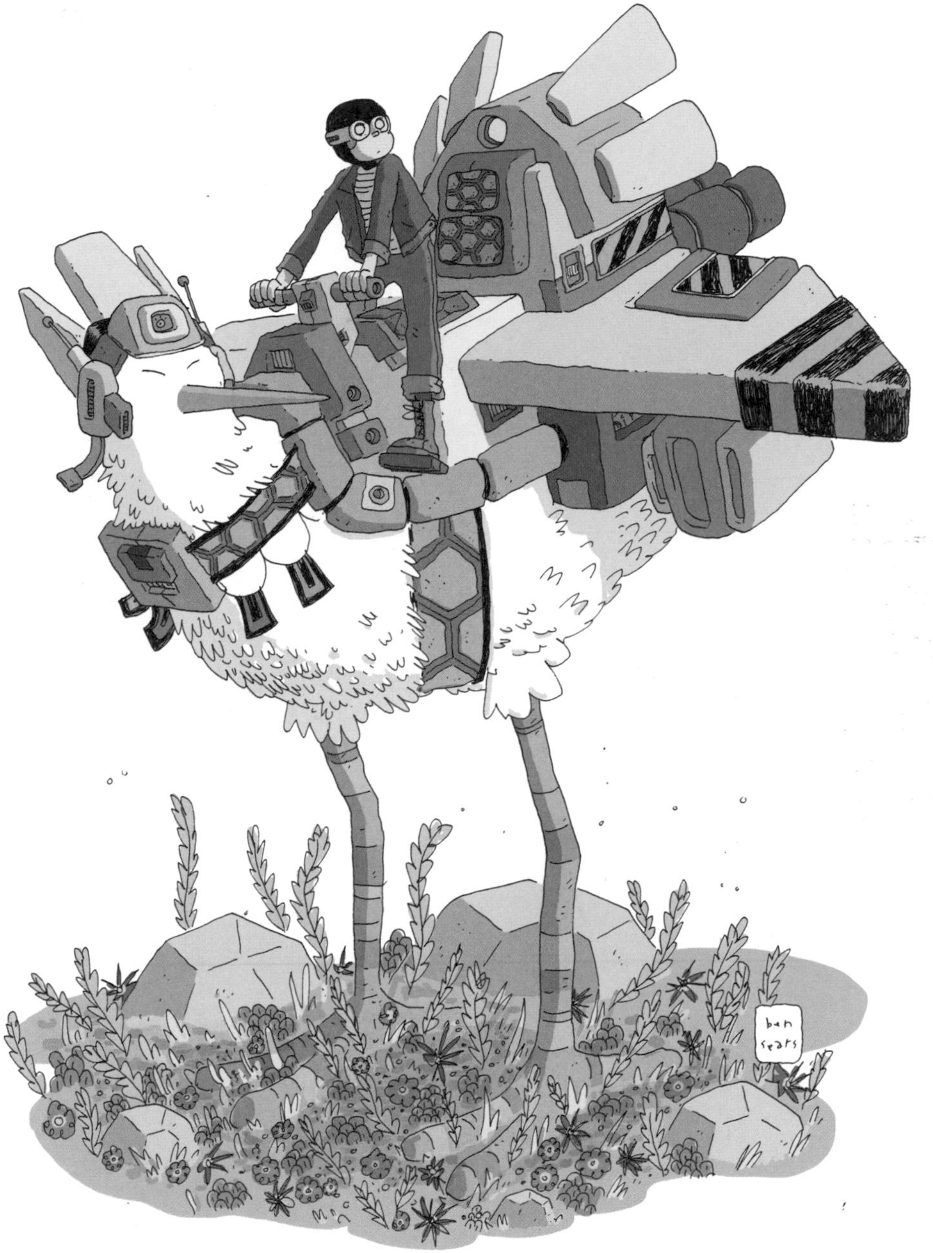
ben sears

ben sears